ABOARD THE TIME SHUTTLE

Two hours passed while the shuttle rushed on into the unexplored and uncharted depths of the Net. I sat watching the fantastic flow of the scenes beyond the view screens—the weird phenomenon that Chief Captain Winter of the TNL Service had called Aentrophy. At the speed at which I was travelling—far greater than anything ever managed by Imperial technicians—living creatures would not be detectable; a man would flash across the screen and be gone in a fraction of a microsecond. But the fixed features of the scene—the streets, the buildings, the stone and metal and wood—loomed around me. And as I watched, they changed . . .

THE OTHER
SIDE OF TIME

KEITH LAUMER

A BERKLEY MEDALLION BOOK
published by
BERKLEY PUBLISHING CORPORATION

COPYRIGHT © 1965, by KEITH LAUMER

*Published by arrangement with
the author's agent*

BERKLEY MEDALLION EDITION, AUGUST, 1965

BERKLEY MEDALLION BOOKS are published by
Berkley Publishing Corporation
15 East 26th Street, New York, N. Y. 10010

Printed in the United States of America

CHAPTER ONE

It was one of those tranquil summer evenings when the sunset colors seemed to linger on in the sky even longer than June in Stockholm could explain. I stood by the French windows, looking out at pale rose and tawny gold and electric blue, feeling a sensation near the back of the neck that always before had meant trouble, big trouble, coming my way.

The phone jangled harshly through the room. I beat the track record getting to it, grabbed the old-fashioned Imperium-style, brass-mounted instrument off the hall table, and waited a moment to be sure my voice wouldn't squeak before I said hello.

"Colonel Bayard?" said the voice at the other end. "The Freiherr von Richthofen calling; one moment, please..."

Through the open archway to the dining room I could see the dark gleam of Barbro's red hair as she nodded at the bottle of wine Luc was showing her. Candlelight from the elaborate chandelier over her head cast a soft light on snowy linen, gleaming crystal, rare old porcelain, glittering silver. With Luc as our household major domo, every meal was an occasion, but my appetite had vanished. I didn't know why. Richthofen was an old and valued friend, as well as the head of Imperial Intelligence....

"Brion?" Richthofen's faintly accented voice came from the bell-shaped earpiece of the telephone. "I am glad to have found you at home."

"What's up, Manfred?"

"Ah..." he sounded mildly embarrassed. "You have been at home all evening?"

"We got in about an hour ago. Have you been trying to reach me?"

"Oh, no. But a small matter has arisen..." There was a pause. "I wonder, Brion, if you could find the time to drop down to Imperial Intelligence Headquarters?"

"Certainly. When?"

"Now. Tonight...." the pause again. Something was bothering him—a strange occurrence in itself. "I'm sorry to disturb you at home, Brion, but—"

"I'll be there in half an hour," I said. "Luc will be unhap-

5

py, but I guess he'll survive. Can you tell me what it's about?"

"I think not, Brion; the wires may not be secure. Please make my apologies to Barbro—and to Luc too."

Barbro had risen and come around the table. "Brion—what was the call—" She saw my face. "Is there trouble?"

"Don't know. I'll be back as soon as I can. It must be important or Manfred wouldn't have called."

I went along the hall to my bedroom, changed into street clothes, took a trench coat and hat—the nights were cool in Stockholm—and went out into the front hall. Luc was there, holding a small apparatus of spring wire and leather.

"I won't be needing that, Luc," I said. "Just a routine trip down to HQ."

"Better take it, sir." Luc's sour face was holding its usual expression of grim dissapproval—an expression I had learned masked an intense loyalty. I grinned at him, took the slug gun and its special quick-draw holster, pulled back my right sleeve and clipped it in place, checked the action. With a flick of the wrist, the tiny slug gun—the shape and color of a flattened, water-eroded stone—slapped into my palm. I tucked it back in place.

"Just to please you, Luc. I'll be back in an hour. Maybe less."

I stepped out into the gleam of the big, square, thick-lensed carriage lights that shed a nostalgic yellow glow over the granite balustrade, went down the wide steps to the waiting car, and slid in behind the thick oak-rimmed wheel. The engine was already idling. I pulled along the gravelled drive, out past the poplars by the open iron gate, into the cobbled city street. Ahead, a car parked at the curb with headlights burning pulled out, took up a position in front of me. In the rearview mirror I saw a second car ease around the corner, fall in behind me. Jeweled highlights glinted from the elaborrate star-burst badge of the Imperial Intelligence bolted to the massive grill. It seemed Manfred had sent along an escort to be sure I made it to headquarters.

It was a ten-minute drive through the wide, softly lit streets of the old capital, superficially like the Stockholm of my native continuum. But here in the Zero-zero world of the Imperium, the center of the vast Net of alternate worlds opened up by the M-C drive, the colors were somehow a little brighter, the evening breeze a little softer, the magic of living a little closer.

Following my escort, I crossed the Norrbro Bridge, made a

6

hard right between red granite pillars into a short drive, swung through a set of massive wrought-iron gates with a wave to the cherry-tunicked sentry as he presented arms. I pulled up before the broad doors of polished ironbound oak and the brass plate that said KUNGLIGA SVENSKA SPIONAGE, and the car behind me braked with a squeal and doors slammed open. By the time I had slid from behind the wheel, the four men from the two cars had formed a casual half-circle around me. I recognized one of them—a Net operative who had chauffeured me into a place called Blight-Insular Two, a few years back. He returned my nod with a carefully impersonal look.

"They're waiting for you in General Baron von Richthofen's suite, Colonel," he said. I grunted and went up the steps, with the curious feeling that my escort was behaving more like a squad of plainclothesmen making a dangerous pinch, than an honor guard.

Manfred got to his feet when I came into the office. The look he gave me was an odd one—as though he weren't quite sure just how to put whatever it was he was about to say.

"Brion, I must ask for your indulgence," he said. "Please take a chair. Something of a . . . a troublesome nature has arisen." He looked at me with a worried expression. This wasn't the suave, perfectly poised von Richthofer I was used to seeing daily in the course of my duties as a colonel of the Imperial Intelligence. I sat, noticing the careful placement of the four armed agents in the room, and the foursome who had walked me to the office, standing silently by.

"Go ahead, sir," I said, getting formal just to keep in the spirit of the thing. "I understand this is business. I assume you'll tell me what it's all about, in time."

"I must ask you a number of questions, Brion," Richthofen said unhappily. He sat down, the lines in his face suddenly showing his nearly eighty years, ran a lean hand over smooth iron grey hair, then straightened himself abruptly, leaned back in the chair with the decisive air of a man who has decided something has to be done and it may as well be gotten over with.

"What was your wife's maiden name?" he rapped out.

"Lundane," I answered levelly. Whatever the game was, I'd play along. Manfred had known Barbro longer than I had. Her father had served with Richthofen as an Imperial agent for thirty years.

7

"When did you meet her?"

"About five years ago—at the Royal Midsummer Ball, the night I arrived here."

"Who else was present that night?"

"You, Hermann Goering, Chief Captain Winter..." I named a dozen of the guests at the gay affair that had ended so tragically with an attack by raiders from the nightmare world known as B-I Two. "Winter was killed," I added, "by a hand grenade that was meant for me."

"What was your work—originally?"

"I was a diplomat—a United States diplomat—until your lads kidnapped me and brought me here." The last was just a subtle reminder that whatever it was that required that my oldest friend in this other Stockholm question me as though I were a stranger, my presence here in the world of the Imperium had been all his idea in the first place. He noted the dig by clearing his throat and twiddling the papers before him for a moment before going on to the next question.

"What is your work here in Stockholm Zero-zero?"

"You gave me a nice job in Intelligence as a Net Surveillance officer—"

"What is the Net?"

"The continuum of alternate world lines; the matrix of simultaneous reality—"

"What is the Imperium?" he cut me off. It was one of those rapid-fire interrogations, designed to rattle the subject and make him forget his lines—not the friendliest kind of questioning a man could encounter.

"The overgovernment of the Zero-zero A-line in which the M-C generator was developed."

"What does M-C abbreviate?"

"Maxoni-Cocini—the boys that invented the thing, back in 1893—"

"How is the M-C effect employed?"

"It's the drive used to power the Net shuttles."

"Where are Net operations carried out?"

"All across the Net—except for the Blight, of course—"

"What is the Blight?"

"Every A-line within thousands of parameters of the Zero-zero line is a hell-world of radiation or—"

"What produced the Blight?"

"The M-C effect, mishandled. You lads here in the Zero-zero line were the only ones who controlled it—"

"What is the Zero-zero line?"

I waved a hand. "This universe we're sitting in right now. The alternate world where the M-C field—"

"Do you have a scar on your right foot?" I smiled—slightly—at the change of pace question.

"Uh-huh. Where Chief Inspector Bale fired a round between my big toe and—"

"Why were you brought here?"

"You needed me to impersonate a dictator—in a place called Blight-Insular Two—"

"Are there other viable A-lines within the Blight?"

I nodded. "Two. One is a war-blasted place with a Common History date of about 1910; the other is my native clime, called B-I Three—"

"You have a bullet scar on your right side?"

"Nope; the left. I also have—"

"What is a Common History date?"

"The date at which two different A-lines' histories diverge—"

"What was your first assignment as a Colonel of Intelligence?"

I answered the question—and a lot of other ones. For the next hour and a half he covered every facet of my private and public life, digging into those odd corners of casual incident that would be known only to me—and to himself. All the while, eight armed men stood by, silent, ready. . . .

My pretense of casual acceptance of the situation was wearing a little thin by the time he sighed, laid both hands on the table—I had the sudden, startled impression that he had just slipped a gun into a drawer out of my line of vision—and looked at me with a more normal expression.

"Brion, in the curious profession of which we are both members one encounters the necessity of performing many unpleasant duties. To call you here like this . . ." he nodded at the waiting gun handlers, who quietly faded away. "Yes, under guard—to question you like a common suspect—has been one of the most unpleasant. Rest assured that it was necessary—and that the question has now been resolved to my complete satisfaction." He rose and extended a hand. I got up, feeling a little suppressed anger trying to bubble up under my collar. I took his hand, shook it once, and dropped it. My reluctance must have showed.

"Later, Brion—perhaps tomorrow—I can explain this farcical affair. For tonight, I ask you to accept my personal apologies for the inconvenience—the embarrassment I have

9

been forced to cause you. It was in the interests of the Imperium."

I made polite but not enthusiastic noises, and left. Whatever it was that was afoot, I knew Richthofen had a reason for what he had done—but that didn't make me like it any better—or reduce my curiosity. But I was damned if I'd ask any questions now.

There was no one in sight as I went along to the elevator, rode down, stepped out into the white marble-paved corridor on the ground floor. Somewhere at the far end of the wide hallway feet were hurrying. A door banged with a curious air of finality. I stood like an animal testing the air before venturing into dangerous new territory. An air of crisis seemed to hang over the silent building.

Then I found myself sniffing in earnest. There was a smell of burning wood and asphalt, a hint of smoke. I turned toward the apparent source, walking rapidly but quietly. I passed the wide foot of the formal staircase that led up to the reception hall one floor above—and halted, swung back, my eyes on a dark smudge against the gleaming white floor tiles. I almost missed the second smudge—a good two yards from the first, and fainter. But the shape of both marks was clear enough: they were footprints. Six feet farther along the corridor there was another faint stain—as though someone had stepped into hot tar, and was tracking it behind him.

The direction of the prints was along the corridor to the left. I looked along the dimly lit way. It all seemed as peaceful as a mortuary after hours—and had that same air of grim business accomplished and more to come.

I went along the hall, paused at the intersection, looking both ways. The odor seemed stronger—a smell like singed paint now. I followed the prints around the corner. Twenty feet along the corridor there was a large burn scar against the floor, with footprints around it—lots of prints. There was also a spatter of blood, and on the wall the bloody print of a hand twice the size of mine. Under a sign that said SERVICE STAIR there was a second hand-print on the edge of a door—a hand-print outlined in blistered, blackened paint. My wrist twitched—a reflex reminder of the slug gun Luc had insisted I bring along.

It was two steps to the door. I reached for the polished brass knob—and jerked my hand back. It was hot to the touch. With my handkerchief wrapped around my hand, I got the door open. Narrow steps went down into shadows and the smell of smouldering wood. I started to reach for the wall switch, then thought better of it, closed the door silently behind me, started down. At the bottom, I waited for a moment, listening, then gingerly poked my head out to look along the dark basement hall—and froze.

Dim shadows danced on the wall opposite—shadows outlined in dull reddish light. I came out, went along to a right-angle turn, risked another look. Fifty feet from me, a glowing figure moved with erratic, jerky speed—a figure that shone in the gloom like a thick-limbed iron statue heated red hot. It darted a few feet, made movements too quick to follow, spun, bobbed across the narrow passage—and disappeared through an open door, like a paper cutout jerked by a string.

My wrist twitched again, and this time the gun was in my hand—a smooth, comforting feeling—nestling against my palm. The odor of smoke was stronger now. I looked down, and in the weak light from behind me made out blackened footprints against the wood plank flooring. The thought occurred to me that I should go back, give an alarm, and then carry on with a few heavily armed guards; but it was just a thought. I was already moving along toward the door, not liking it very well, but on the trail of something that wouldn't wait.

The odor was thick in the air now. The hot cloth smell of a press-'em-while-you-wait shop, mingled with the hot metallic tang of a foundry, and a little autumnal woodsmoke thrown in for balance. I came up smooth and silent to the door, flattened myself against the wall, covered the last few inches like a caterpillar sneaking up on a tender young leaf. I risked a fast look inside. The glow from the phantom intruder threw strange reddish shadows on the walls of an unused storeroom —dusty, dark, scattered with odds and ends of litter that should have been swept up but hadn't.

In the center of the room, the fiery man himself leaned over a sprawled body—a giant figure in a shapeless coverall. The fiery man's hands—strange, glowing hands in clumsy looking gauntlets—plucked at his victim with more-than-human dexterity; then he straightened. I didn't take time to goggle at the spectacle of a three-hundred-degree centigrade murderer. There was a chance that his victim wasn't dead yet—and if I hit him quick enough to capitalize on the tiny advantage of surprise . . .

I forgot all about the slug gun. I went through the door at

11

a run, launched myself at the figure from whom heat radiated like a tangible wall and saw it turn with unbelievable, split-second speed, throw up a hand—five glowing fingers outspread—take one darting step back—

Long, pink sparks crackled from the outflung hand, leaping toward me. Like a diver hanging suspended in midair, I saw the harsh electric glare, heard the *pop!* as the miniature lightnings closed with me. . . .

Then a silent explosion turned the world to blinding white, hurling me into nothingness.

For a long time I lay, clinging to the dim and formless dream that was my refuge from the hazy memory of smouldering footprints, a deserted room, and a fantastic glowing man crouched over his victim. I groaned, groped for the dream again, found only hard, cold concrete against my face, a roiling nausea in the pit of my stomach, and a taste like copper pennies in my mouth. I found the floor, pushed hard to get my face up out of the grit, blinked gummed eyes . . .

The room was dark, silent, dusty and vacant as a robbed grave. I used an old tennis shoe someone had left in my mouth as a tongue, grated it across dry lips, made the kind of effort that under other circumstances had won luckier souls the Congressional Medal, and sat up. There was a ringing in my head like the echo of the Liberty Bell just before it cracked.

I maneuvered to hands and knees, and, taking it by easy stages, got to my feet. I sniffed. The burning odor was gone like the crease in four dollar pants. And my quarry hadn't waited around to see whether I was all right. He—or it—had been gone for some time—and had taken the corpse with him.

The light in the room was too weak to show me any detail. I fumbled, got out a massive flint and steel Imperium-style lighter, made three tries, got a smoky yellow flame and squinted to find the trail of blackened prints that would show me which way the fiery man had gone.

There weren't any.

I went all the way to the door, looking for the scars I had seen earlier, then came back, cast about among empty cardboard cartons and stacked floor wax drums. There were no footprints—not even the old-fashioned kind—except for mine. The dust was thick, undisturbed. There were no marks to show where the body had lain, not a trace of my wild charge across the room. Only the scrabble marks I had made getting to my feet proved that I wasn't dreaming my own existence. I had heard of people who pinched themselves to see if they were dreaming. It had always seemed a little silly to me—you could dream a pinch as well as any other, more soothing, sensation. But I solemnly took a fold of skin on the back of my hand, squeezed hard. I could barely feel it.

That didn't seem to prove anything one way or another. I made it to the door like a man walking to the undertaker's to save that last cab fare, and went into the hall. The lights were out. Only a dim, phosphorescent glow seemed to emanate from the walls and floor. The sight of the wood planking gave me no comfort at all. The prints burned here had been dark, distinct, charred. Now the dull varnish gleamed at me, unmarked.

The buzzing in my head had diminished to a faint hum, like that of a trapped fly, as I pushed through the door into the ground floor hallway. The milk glass globe hanging from the high ceiling glared at me with an unhealthy electric blue. A blackish haze seemed to hang in the still air of the silent corridor, lending a funereal tinge to the familiar vista of marble floor and varnished doors. Behind me, the door clicked shut with a shockingly loud, metallic clatter. I took a few breaths of the blackish air, failed to detect any hint of smoke. A glance at the door showed me what I had expected —smooth dark brown paint, unmarked by burning hand-prints.

I crossed the hall, pushed into an empty office. On the desk, a small clay pot sat on a blotter, filled with hard, baked-looking dirt. One dry leaf lay on the desk beside it. The desk clock said twelve-oh-five. I reached past it, picked up the phone, jiggled the hook. The silence at the other end was like a concrete wall. I jiggled some more, failed to evoke so much as a crackle of line static. I left the room, tried the next office with the same result. The phones were as dead as my hopes of living to a ripe old age outside a padded cell.

My footsteps in the corridor had a loud, clattering quality. I made it to the front entrance, pushed out through the heavy door, stood on the top step looking down at my car, still sitting where I had left it. The two escort vehicles were gone. Beyond the car, I noticed that the guard shack at the gate was dark. The street lamps seemed to be off too, and the usual gay pattern of the lights of the city's towers was missing. But a power failure wouldn't affect the carbide pole lights. . . . My glance went on to the sky; it was black, overcast. Even the stars were in on the black out.

I got into the car, turned the switch and pressed the starter button on the floor. Nothing happened. I muttered an impolite suggestion, tried again. No action. The horn didn't work either, and twisting the light switch produced nothing but a dry *snick!*

I got out of the car, stood undecided for a moment, then started around the building for the garages in the rear. I slowed, halted before I got there. They were dark, the heavy doors closed and barred. I fetched up another sigh, and for the first time noticed the dead, stale smell of the air. I walked back along the drive, passed the guard post, unaccountably deserted, emerged onto the street. It stretched into shadows, silent and dark. Predictably, there were no cabs in sight. A few cars stood at the curb. I started off toward the bridge, noticed a dark shape halfway across it: a car, without lights, parked midway in the span. For some reason, the sight shocked me. A small, uneasy feeling began to supplant the irritated frustration that had been gathering strength somewhere down below my third shirt button. I walked along to the car, peered in through the rolled up windows. There was no one inside. I thought of pushing the car to the side of the street, then considered the state of my constitution at the moment and went on.

There were more abandoned cars in Gustav Adolfstorg, all parked incongruously in midstream. One was a boxy, open touring car. The ignition switch was on, and the light switch too. I went on, checked the next one I came to. The switches were on. It appeared that there had been an epidemic of automotive ignition trouble in the city tonight, as well as a breakdown in the power plants—a coincidence that did nothing to improve my spirits.

I walked on across the square with its heroic equestrian statue, past the dark front of the Opera House, crossed Arsenalsgatan, turned up Tradgarsgatan, walked past shuttered shops, bleak in an eerie light like that of an eclipse. The city was absolutely still. No breeze stirred the lifeless air, no growl of auto engines disturbed the silence, no clatter of feet, no distant chatter of voices. My first faint sense of uneasiness was rapidly developing into a full-scale cold sweat.

I cut across the corner of the park, skirting the glass display

14

cases crowded with provincial handicrafts, and hurried across a stretch of barren clay.

The wrongness of it penetrated my preoccupation. I looked back across the expanse of sterile earth, searching on across the garden—the oddly naked garden. There were the gravelled paths, the tile lined pools—their fountaining jets lifeless—the band shell, the green painted benches, the steel lampposts with their attached refuse containers and neatly framed tram schedules. But not one blade of grass, not a tree or flowering shrub—no sign of the magnificent bed of prize rhododendron that had occupied a popular magazine's rotogravure section only a week earlier. I turned and started on, half-running now, the unease turning to an undefined dread that caught at my throat and surged in my stomach like foul water in a foundering galley's bilge.

I pushed through the iron gates of my house, wheezing like a blown boiler from the run. I stared at the blank black windows, feeling the implacable air of abandonment, desolation—of utter vacantness. I went on up the drive, taking in the bare stretch of dirt that had been verdant only hours before. Where the poplars had stood, curious foot-wide pits showed black against the grey soil. Only a scatter of dead leaves was left to remind me that once trees had stood here. The crunch of my feet on the gravel was loud. I stepped off onto the former lawn, felt my feet sink into the dry, crumbling earth. At the steps, I looked back. Only my trail of footmarks showed that life had ever existed here—those, and a scatter of dead insects under the carriage lamps. The door opened. I pushed inside, stood savoring the funereal hush, my heart thudding painfully, high in my chest.

"Barbro!" I called. My voice was a dry croak—a croak of cold fear. I ran along the unlighted hall, went up the stairs four at a time, slammed through the sitting room door, on through into the bedroom. I found only silence, an aching stillness in which the sounds of my passage seemed to echo with a shocked reproach. I stumbled out of the room, yelling for Luc, not really expecting an answer now, yelling to break the awful, ominous stillness, the fear of what I might find in the dark, dead rooms.

I searched room by room, went back and tried the closets, shouting, slamming doors wide, not fighting the panic that was welling up inside me, but giving it vent in violent action.

There was nothing. Every room was in perfect order, every

15

piece of furniture in its accustomed place, every drape discreetly drawn, every dish and book and garment undisturbed—but on the marble mantelpiece, the brass clock sat silent, its tick stilled. And in the pots where the broad-leafed plants had lent their touch of green, only the dead soil remained. I stood in the center of the dark library, staring out at the grim, metallic glow of the night sky, feeling the silence flow back in like a tangible thing, trying now to regain my control, to accept the truth: Barbro was gone—along with every other living thing in the Imperial capital.

CHAPTER TWO

I didn't notice the sound at first. I was sitting in the empty drawing room, staring out past the edge of heavy brocaded drapes at the empty street, listening to the thud of my empty heart. . . .

Then it penetrated: a steady thumping, faint, far away—but a sound—in the silent city. I jumped up, made it to the door and was out on the steps before the idea of caution occurred to me. The thumping was clearer now: a rhythmic slap, like the feet of marching troops, coming closer—

I saw them then, a flicker of movement through the iron spears of the fence. I faded back inside, watched from the darkness as they swung past, four abreast, big men in drab, shapeless coveralls. I tried to estimate their number. Perhaps two hundred, some laden with heavy packs, some with rifle-like weapons, one or two being helped by their comrades. They'd seen action somewhere tonight.

The last of them passed, and I ran softly down the drive. Keeping to the shelter of the buildings along the avenue, I followed a hundred yards behind them.

The first, stunning blow was past now, leaving me with a curious sense of detachment. The detachment of the sole survivor. The troop ahead swung along Nybroviken, grim, high-shouldered marchers a head taller than my six feet, not singing, not talking—just marching, block after block, past empty cars, empty buildings, empty parks—and a dead cat, lying in the gutter. I paused, stared at the ruffled, pathetic cadaver.

They turned left into Uppsalavägen—and I realized then where they were headed—to the Net Terminus Building at

Stallmästaregården. I was watching from the shelter of a massive oak a hundred yards away as the end of the column turned in at the ornate gate, and disappeared beyond the massive portal that had been smashed from its hinges. One man dropped off, took up a post at the entry.

I crossed the street silently, followed the walk around to the side entrance, wasted a few seconds wishing for the keys in my safe back at the house, then headed for the back of the building. Stumbling through denuded flower beds, I followed the line of the wall, barely visible in the blackish light—a light that seemed, curiously, to shine upward from the ground rather than impinge from the starless sky. A masonry wall barred my way. I jumped, caught the top edge, pulled myself over, dropped into the paved court behind the Terminal. Half a dozen boxy wheeled shuttles were parked here, of the special type used for work in some of the nearer A-lines—worlds with Common History dates only a few centuries in the past, where other Stockholms existed with streets in which a disguised delivery van could move unnoticed.

One of the vehicles was close to the building wall. I climbed up on its hood, reached, tried to lift the wide, metal framed, double-hung window. It didn't budge. I went back down, fumbled in the dark under the shuttle's dash, brought out the standard tool kit, found a hammer, scrambled back up, and as gently as I could, smashed the glass from the frame. It made a hell of a racket. I stood listening, half expecting to hear indignant voices calling questions, but the only sound was my own breathing, and a creak from the shuttle's springs as I shifted my weight.

The room I clambered into was a maintenance shop, lined with long workbenches littered with disassembled shuttle components, its walls hung with tools and equipment. I went out through the door at the far end of the room, along the corridor to the big double doors leading into the garages. Faint sounds came from within. I eased the door open a foot, slipped inside, into the echoing stillness of the wide, high vaulted depot. A double row of Net shuttles reared up in the gloom—heavy, ten-man machines, smaller three-man scouts, a pair of light new-model single-seaters at the far end of the line.

And beyond them—dwarfing them—a row of dark blocky machines of strange design, massive and ugly as garbage scows, illogically dumped here among the elegantly decorated vehicles of the Imperial TNL service. Dark figures moved

17

around the strange machines, forming up into groups beside each heavy transport, responding to gestures and an occasional grunted command. I walked along behind the parked shuttles, eased forward between two from which I had a clear view of the proceedings.

The doors of the first of the five alien machines were open. As I watched, a suited man clambered in, followed by the next in line. The troops—whoever they were—were reembarking. They were clumsy, slope-shouldered heavyweights, covered from head to toe in baggy, dull grey suits with dark glass faceplates. One of the Imperial machines was impeding the smooth flow of the moving column; two of the intruders stepped to it, gripped it by its near side runner, and, with one heave, tipped it up, dumped it over on its side with a heavy slam and a tinkle of breaking glass. I felt myself edging farther back out of sight; the scout weighed a good two tons.

The first shuttle was loaded now. The line of men shuffled along to the next and continued loading. Time was slipping past. In another ten minutes all the suited men would be aboard their machines, gone—back to whatever world-line they had come from. It was clear that these were invaders from the Net—a race of men, unknown to Imperial authorities, who possessed an M-C drive of their own. Men who were my only link with the vanished inhabitants of desolated Stockholm Zero-zero. Waiting here wouldn't help; I had to follow them, learn what I could. . . .

I took a bracing lungful of the stale Terminal air and stepped out of my hiding place, feeling as exposed as a rat between holes as I moved along the wall, putting distance between myself and the strangers. My objective was one of the two-man scouts—a fast, maneuverable machine with adequate armament and the latest in instrumentation. I reached it, got the door open with no more than a rattle of the latch that sent my stomach crowding up under my ribs; but there was no alarm.

Even inside, there was enough of the eerie light to see my way by. I went forward to the control compartment, slid into the operator's seat, and tried the main drive warm-up switch.

Nothing happened. I tried other controls, without response. The M-C drive was as dead as the cars abandoned in the city streets. I got up, went back to the entry and eased it open, stepped silently out. I could hear the invaders working away two hundred feet from me, shielded from view by the ranked

18

shuttles. An idea was taking form—an idea I didn't like very well. The first thing it would require was that I get around to the opposite side of the Terminal. I turned . . .

He was standing ten feet away, just beyond the rear corner of the shuttle. At close range he looked seven feet tall, wide in proportion, with gloved hands the size of briefcases. He took a step toward me, and I backed away. He followed, almost leisurely. Two more steps and I would be clear of the shelter of the machine, exposed to the view of any of the others who might happen to glance my way. I stopped. The stranger kept on coming, one immense, stubby-fingered hand reaching for me.

My wrist twitched, and the slug gun was in my hand. I aimed for a point just below the center of the chest, and fired. At the muffled *slap!* of the gun, the monster-man jacknifed, went down backward with a slam like a horse falling in harness. I jumped past him to the shelter of the next machine, and crouched there, waiting. It seemed impossible that no one had heard the shot or the fall of the victim, but the sounds from the far end of the vast shed went on, uninterrupted. I let out a breath I just realized I had been holding, feeling my heart thumping in my chest like a trapped rabbit's.

With the gun still in my hand, I stepped out, went back to the man I had shot. He lay on his back, spread-eagled like a bearskin rug—and about the same size. Through his shattered faceplate, I saw a broad, coarse, dead-grey face, with porous skin, and a wide, lipless mouth, half-open now to show square, yellow teeth. Small eyes, pale blue as a winter sky, stared lifelessly under bushy yellow brows that grew in a continuous bar across the forehead. A greasy lock of dull blonde hair fell beside one hollow temple. It was the most appallingly hideous face I had ever seen. I backed off from it, turned and started off into the shadows.

The last in line of the alien shuttles was my target. To get to it, I had to cross an open space of perhaps fifty feet, concealed by nothing but the dimness of the light. I stepped out, started across the exposed stretch as silently as slick leather soles would let me. Every time one of them turned in my direction, I froze until he turned away. I had almost reached shelter when one of the officers tallying men turned to stare toward the other end of the huge shed. Someone had missed the one I had shot. The officer called—a sudden hoarse cry like a bellow of mortal agony. The others paid no attention. The officer snapped an order, started off to investigate.

I had perhaps half a minute before he found his missing crewman. I slipped into the shadow of the supply shuttle, worked my way quickly to the last in line, slid around the end. The coast was clear. I made it to the entry in three quick steps, swung myself up, and stepped inside the enemy machine.

There was a sickish animal odor here, a subtle alienness of proportion. I took in the control panels, the operator's chair, the view-screens, and the chart table in a swift glance. All were recognizable—but in size and shape and detail they differed in a hundred ways from the familiar Imperial patterns, or from any normal scheme of convenience. I hitched myself into the high, wide, hard seat, stared at squares and circles of plastic glowing in clashing shades of brown and violet. Curious symbols embossed on metal strips labelled some of the baroquely curved levers which projected from the dull ochre panel. A pair of prominent foot pedals, set awkwardly wide apart, showed signs of heavy wear.

I stared at the array, feeling the sweat begin to pop out on my forehead. I had only a few seconds to decide—and if my guess were wrong—

A simple knife switch set in the center of the panel drew my attention. There were scratches on the panel around it, and worn spots on the mud-colored plastic grip. It was as good a guess as any. I reached out tentatively—

Outside, a horrific shriek ripped through the silence. I jerked, smashing my knee against a sharp corner of the panel. The pain brought a warm flood of instinctive anger and decision. I ground my teeth together, reached again, slammed the lever down.

At once, the lights dimmed. I heard the entry close with an echoing impact. Heavy vibration started up, rattling ill-fitting panel members. Indicator lights began to wink; curious lines danced on a pair of glowing pinkish screens. I felt a ghostly blow against the side of the hull. One of the boys wanted in, but he was a trifle too late. The screens had cleared to show me a view of black desolation under a starless sky—the familiar devastation of the Blight. The M-C field was operating; the stolen shuttle was carrying me out across the Net of alternate worlds—and at terrific speed, to judge from the quicksilver flow of the scene outside as I flashed across the parallel realities of the A-lines. I had made my escape. The next order of business was to determine how to control the strange machine.

Half an hour's study of the panel sufficed to give me a general idea of the meanings of the major instruments. I was ready now to attempt to maneuver the stolen shuttle. I gripped the control lever, tugged at it—it didn't move. I tried again, succeeded only in bending the metal arm. I stood, braced my feet, put my shoulders into it. With a sharp clang, the lever broke off short. I sank back in the chair, tossed the broken handle to the floor. Evidently, the controls were locked. The owners of the strange shuttle had taken precautions against any disgruntled potential deserter who might have an impulse to ride the machine to some idyllic world line of his own choice. Once launched, its course was predetermined, guided by automatic instruments—and I was powerless to stop it.

CHAPTER THREE

Two hours passed while the shuttle rushed on into the unexplored and uncharted depths of the Net. I sat watching the fantastic flow of scenes beyond the view screens—the weird phenomenon that Chief Captain Winter of the TNL Service had called A-entropy. At the speed at which I was travelling —far greater than anything ever managed by Imperial technicians—living creatures would not be detectable; a man would flash across the screen and be gone in a fraction of a microsecond. But the fixed features of the scene—the streets, the buildings, the stone and metal and wood—loomed around me. And as I watched, they changed. . . .

The half-familiar structures seemed to flow, to shrink or expand gradually, sprouting outré new elements. I saw doorways widen, or dwindle and disappear; red granite blocks rippled and flowed, changed by degrees to grey polished slabs. The nearly legible lettering on a nearby shop window writhed, reformed itself, the Roman capitals distorting into forms like Cyrillic letters, then changed again, and again, to become lines of meaningless symbols. I saw sheds and shacks appear and swell, crowding among the older structures, burgeoning mightily into blank, forbidding piles that soared up out of sight. Balconies budded as window ledges, grew into great cantilevered terraces, then merged, shutting out the sky—and then they, in turn, drew back, and new façades stood revealed:

21

grim, blackish ribbed columns, rearing up a thousand feet into the unchanging sky, linked by narrow bridges that shifted, twitching like nervous fingers, widening, spreading into a vast network that entangled the spires like a spider's web, then broke, faded back, leaving only a dark bar here and there to join the now ponderous squat towers like chains linking captive monsters. All this in a frozen, eternal instant of time, as the stolen shuttle rushed blindly across the lines of alternate probability toward its unknown destination.

I sat entranced, watching the universe evolve around me. Then I found myself nodding, my eyes aching abominably. I suddenly realized that I hadn't eaten my dinner yet—nor slept —in how many hours? I got out of the chair, made a quick search of the compartment, and found a coarse-woven cloak with a rank odor like attar of locker room blended with essence of stable. I was too weary to be choosy, though. I spread the cloth on the floor in the tiny space between the operator's seat and the power compartment, curled up on it, and let the overwhelming weariness sweep over me. . . .

. . . and awakened with a start. The steady drone of the drive had changed in tone, dropped to a deep thrumming. My watch said I'd been on the way a little less than three and a half hours—but brief as the trip had been, the ugly but fantastically efficient shuttle had raced across the Net into regions where the Imperial scouts had never penetrated. I scrambled up, got my eyes open far enough to make out the screens.

It was a scene from a drunk's delirium. Strange, crooked towers rose up from dark, empty canyons where footpaths threaded over heaped refuse among crowded stalls, doorless arches, between high-wheeled carts laden with meaningless shapes of wood and metal and leather. From carved stone lintels, cornices, pilasters, grotesque faces peered, goggled, grimaced like devils in an Aztec tomb. As I gaped, the growl of the drive sank to a mutter, died. The oddly shifting scene froze into the immobility of identity. I had arrived—somewhere.

But the street—if I could use that term for this crowded alley—was deserted, and the same odd, fungoid light I had seen in the empty streets of Stockholm glowed faintly from every surface under the dead, empty, opaque blackness of the sky above.

Then without warning a wave of nausea bent me double, retching. The shuttle seemed to rise under me, twist, spin. Forces seized me, stretched me out as thin as copper wire,

22

threaded me through the red-hot eye of a needle, then slammd me into a compacted lump like a metal-baler cubing a junked car. I heard a whistling noise, and it was me, trying to get enough air into my lungs to let out a yell of agony—

And then the pressure was gone. I was sprawled on my back on the hard floor, but still breathing and in my usual shape, watching lights wink out on the panel. I felt the sharp, reassuring pain of an honest cut on my knee, saw a small dark patch of blood through a tear in the cloth. I got to my feet, and the screen caught my eye. . . .

The two-foot rectangle of the view-plate showed me a crowd packing the narrow street that had been deserted a moment ago. A mob of squat, hulking, long-armed creatures surging and milling in an intricate play of dark and light where vivid shafts of sunlight struck down from high above into deep shadow—

Then behind me metal growled. I whirled, saw the entry hatch jump, swing open. The shuttle trembled, lurched—and a vast, wide shape stepped in through the opening—a fanged monstrosity with a bulging, bald head, a wide, thin-lipped, chinless face, huge, strangely elaborate ears, a massive, hulking body buckled into straps and hung with clanking bangles, incongruous against a shaggy pelt like a blonde gorilla's.

The muscles of my right wrist tensed, ready to slap the slug gun into my hand, but I relaxed, let my arms fall to my sides. I could kill this fellow—and the next one who stepped inside. But there was more at stake here than my own personal well-being. A moment before, I had seen the miracle of a deserted street transformed in the wink of an eye into a teeming marketplace packed with sunlight and movement. If these grotesque, golden-haired apes knew the secret of that enchantment then maybe my own Stockholm could also come back from the dead . . . if I could find the secret.

"All right, big boy," I said aloud. "I'll come along peacefully."

The creature reached, clamped a hand like a power shovel on my shoulder, literally lifted me, and hurled me at the door. I struck the jamb, bounced, fell out into an odor like dead meat and broccoli rotting together. A growl ran through the shaggy mob surrounding me. They jumped back, jabbering. I made it to my feet, slapping at the decayed rubbish clinging to my jacket, and my captor came up from behind, grabbed my arm as though he had decided to tear it off, and sent me

23

spinning ahead. I hooked a foot in a loop of melon rind, went down again. Something hit me across the back of the shoulders like a falling tree. I oofed, tried to get to hands and knees to make my white god speech, and felt a kick that slammed me forward, my face ploughing into spongy, reeking garbage. I came up spitting, in time to take a smashing blow full in the face, and saw bright constellations burst above me, like a Fourth of July display long ago in another world.

I was aware of my feet dragging, and worked them to relieve the gouging of hard fingers under my arms. Then I was stumbling, half dragged between two of the hairy men, who shouldered their way through the press of babbling spectators that gave way reluctantly, their eyes like blue marbles staring at me as though I were a victim of a strange and terrible disease.

It seemed like a long way that they hauled me, while I gradually adjusted my thinking to the reality of my captivity by creatures that awakened racial memories of ogres and giants and things that went bump in the night. But here they were, as real as life and twice as smelly, scratching at hairy hides with fingers like bananas, showing great yellowish fighting fangs in grimaces of amazement and disgust, and looming over me like angry goblins over a small boy. I stumbled along through the hubbub of raucous sound and eye-watering stench toward whatever fate trolls kept in store for mortals who fell among them.

We came out from the narrow way into a wider but not cleaner avenue lined with curious, multitiered stalls, where grey-maned merchants squatted, peering down from their high perches, shouting their wares, tossing down purchases to customers, catching thick, square coins on the fly. There were heaped fruits, odd-shaped clay pots of all sizes capped and sealed with purplish tar, drab-colored mats of woven fiber, flimsy-looking contraptions of hammered sheet metal, harnesses, straps of leather with massive brass buckles, strings of brightly polished brass and copper discs like old English horse brasses.

And in this fantastic bazaar a horde of variegated near-humanity milled. A dozen races and colors of shaggy sub-men, half-men, ape-men: man-like giants with great bushes of bluish hair fringing bright red faces; incredibly tall, slim creatures, with sleek, black fur, curiously short legs and long, flat feet; wide, squat individuals with round shoulders and long, drooping noses. Some wore great loops and strings of the

24

polished brasses, others had only one or two baubles pinned to the leather straps that seemed to constitute their only clothing. And others, the more bedraggled members, with strap-worn shoulders and horny bare feet, had no brass at all. And over all, great blue and green flies hovered, droning, like a living canopy.

I saw the crowd part to let a great, slow-moving beast push through, a thing as big as a small Indian elephant, and with the same ponderous tread; but the trunk was no more than an exaggerated pig's snout, and from below it two great shovel tusks of yellow ivory thrust out from the underslung jaw above a drooping pink lower lip, looped with saliva and froth. Wide strips of inch-thick leather harnessed the beast to a heavy cart stacked with hooped barrels, and a shaggy driver atop the load slapped a vast braided whip across the massive back of his animal. Farther on, two of the short, burly man-things—they would weigh in at five hundred pounds apiece, I estimated—toiled in harness beside a mangy mastodon-like animal whose blunt tusks were capped with six-inch wooden knobs.

We reached the end of the boulevard and after a short delay to kick a few determined spectators back, my bodyguard urged me roughly up a wide, garbage-littered flight of steep, uneven stone steps—on through a gaping, doorless opening where two lowbrowed louts in black straps and enamelled brasses rose from crouching positions to intercept us. I leaned on the wall and worked on getting my arms back into their sockets while the boys staged a surly reunion. Other members emerged from the hot, zoo-smelling gloom of the rabbit warren building; they came over to wrinkle brows and grimace at me, prodding and poking with fingers like gun barrels. I backed away, flattened myself against the wall, remembering, for some unfortunate reason, a kitten that Gargantua had been very fond of until it broke. . . .

My guards pushed through, clamped onto my arms again in a proprietary way, hooted for gangway, and dragged me into one of the arched openings off the irregularly-shaped entry hall. I tried to follow the turnings and twisting and dips and rises of the tunnel-like passage with some vague idea of finding my way back later, but I soon lost track. It was almost pitch dark here. Small, yellowish incandescent bulbs glowed at fifty-foot intervals, showing me a puddled floor, and rough-hewn walls with many branching side passages. After a couple of hundred yards, the hall widened into a gloomy thirty-foot chamber. One of my keepers, rooted in a heap of rubbish, produced a wide strap of thick blackish leather attached to the wall by a length of rope. He buckled it around my right wrist, gave me a shove, then went and squatted by the wall. The other cop went off along a corridor that curved sharply up and out of sight. I kicked enough of the damp debris aside to make a place to sit, and settled down for a wait. Sooner or later someone in authority would be wanting to interrogate me. For that, communication would have to be established—and as a Net-travelling race, I assumed my captors would have some linguistic capability. After that . . .

I remember stretching out full length on the filthy floor, having a brief thought that for slimy brick, it was amazingly comfortable; then a big, hard foot was kicking at me. I started to sit up, was hauled to my feet by the rope on my arm, and marched along another dingy passage. My feet were almost too heavy to lift now, and my stomach felt like a raw wound. I tried to calculate how many hours it had been since I had eaten, but lost count. My brain was working sluggishly, like a clock dipped in syrup.

The chamber we arrived at—somewhere high in the squat building, I thought; the walk had been mostly along upward-slanting corridors—was domed, roughly circular, with niches set in the irregularly-surfaced walls. There was a terrible odor of dung and rotting hay. The room seemed more like a den in a zoo than an apartment in a human dwelling. I had an impulse to look around for the opening the bear would emerge from.

There were heaps of greyish rags dumped in some of the niches. One of them moved, and I realized that it was a living creature—an incredibly aged, scruffy specimen of my captors' race. The two escorting me urged me closer to the ancient. They had a subdued air now, as though in the presence of rank. In the poor light that filtered in from an arrangement of openings around the walls, I saw a hand like a grey leather-covered claw come up, rake fitfully at the thin, moth-eaten chest hair of the oldster. I made out his eyes then—dull blue, half-veiled by drooping upper lids, nested in the bloodred crescents of sagging lower lids. They stared at me fixedly, unblinking. Below, great tufts of grey hair sprouted from gaping half-inch nostrils. The mouth was puckered, toothless, as wide as a hip pocket. The rest of the face was a mass of doughy wrinkles, framed between long locks of uncombed white hair from which incredible long-lobed ears poked, obscenely pink and naked. The chin hair, caked with foreign matter, hung down across the shrunken chest, against which bony, bald knees poked up like grey stones. I accidentally breathed, choked at a stench like a rotting whale, and was jerked back into position.

The patriarch made a hoarse, croaking noise. I waited, breathing through my mouth. One of my jailers shook me, barked something at me.

"Sorry, fellows," I croaked. "No kapoosh."

The bearded elder jumped as though he'd been poked with a hot iron. He squalled something, spraying me in the process. He bounced up and down with surprising energy, still screeching, then stopped abruptly and thrust his face close to mine. One of my guards grabbed my neck with a hard hand, anticipating my reaction. I stared into the blue eyes—eyes as human as mine, set in this ghastly caricature of a face—saw the open pores as big as match heads, watched a trickle of saliva find its way from the loose mouth down into the beard. . . .

He leaned back with a snuffle, waved an arm, made a speech. When he finished, a thin voice piped up from the left. I twisted, saw another mangy bearskin rug shifting position. My owners propelled me in that direction, held me while the second oldster, even uglier than the first, looked me over. While he stared and drooled, my gaze wandered up to a higher niche. In the shadows, I could barely make out the propped bones of a skeleton, the empty eye sockets gazing down, the massive jaws grinning sardonically, a thick leather strap still circling the neck bones. Apparently promotion to the local Supreme Court was a life appointment.

A jerk at my arm brought me back to more immediate matters. The grandpa before me shrilled. I didn't answer. He curled his lips back, exposing toothless yellowish gums and a tongue like a pink sock full of sand, and screamed. That woke up a couple more wise men; there were answering hoots and squawks from several directions.

My keepers dutifully guided me over to the next judge, an obese old fellow with a bloated, sparsely-haired belly over which large black fleas hurried on erratic paths like bloodhounds looking for a lost trail. This one had one tooth left—a hooked, yellow-brown canine over an inch long. He showed it to me, made gobbling noises, then leaned out and took a swipe at me with an arm as long as a dock crane. My alert guardians pulled me back as I ducked; I was grateful; even this senile old reprobate packed enough wallop to smash my jaw and break my neck if he had connected.

At a querulous cry from a niche high up in a dark corner, we steered in that direction. A lank hand with two fingers missing groped, pulled a crooked body up into a sitting position. Half a face looked down at me. There were scars, then a ragged edge, then bare, exposed bone where the right cheek had been. The eye socket was still there, but empty, the lid puckered and sunken. The mouth, with one corner missing, failed to close properly—an effect that produced a vacuous, loose-lipped smile—as appropriate to this horror as a poodle shave on a hyena.

I was staggering now, not reacting as promptly as my leaders would have liked. The one on the left—the more vicious of the two, I had already decided—lifted me up by one arm, slammed me down, jerked me back to my feet, then shook me like a dusty blanket. I staggered, got my feet back under me, jerked free, and hit him hard in the belly. It was like punching a sandbag; he twisted me casually back into position. I don't think he even noticed the blow.

We stood in the center of the room for a while then, while the council of elders deliberated. One got mad and spat across the room at the big-bellied one, who replied with a hurled handful of offal. Apparently that was the sign for the closing of the session. My helpers backed off, shoved me out into the corridor, and hustled me off on another trip through the crooked passages, with hoots and snarls ringing from the chamber behind us.

This journey ended in still another room, like the others no more than a wide place in the corridor. There was a stone bench, some crude-looking shelves big enough for coffins in one corner, the usual dim bulb, heaped garbage, and odds and ends of equipment of obscure function. There was a hole in the center of the chamber from which a gurgling sound came. Sanitary facilities, I judged, from the odor. This time I was strapped by one ankle and allowed to sit on the floor. A clay pot with some sort of mush in it was thrust at me. I got a whiff, gagged, pushed it away. I wasn't that hungry—not yet.

An hour passed. I had the feeling I was waiting for something. My two proprietors—or two others, I wasn't sure—sat across the room, hunkered down on their haunches, dipping up their dinner from their food pots, not talking. I could hardly smell the place now—my olfactory nerves were numb.

Every so often a newcomer would shamble in, come over to gape at me, then move off.

Then a messenger arrived, barked something peremptory. My escorts got to their feet, licked their fingers carefully with thick, pink tongues as big as shoe soles, came over and unstrapped the ankle bracelet, and started me off again. We went down, this time—taking one branching byway after another, passing through a wide hall where at least fifty hulking louts sat at long benches, holding some sort of meeting, past an entry through which late evening light glowed, then down again, into a narrow passage that ended in a cul-de-sac.

Lefty—my more violent companion—yanked at my arm, thrust me toward a round, two-foot opening, like an oversized rat-hole, set eighteen inches above the floor. It was just about wide enough for a man to crawl into. I got the idea. For a moment, I hesitated; this looked like the end of the trail. Once inside, there'd be no further opportunities for escape—not that I had had any so far.

A blow on the side of the head slammed me against the wall. I went down, twisted on my back. The one who had hit me was standing over me, reaching for a new grip. I'd had about enough of this fellow. Without pausing to consider the consequences, I bent my knee, smashed a hard, ikedo-type kick to his groin. He doubled over, and my second kick caught him square in the mouth. I got a glimpse of pinkish blood welling—

The other man-ape grabbed me, thrust me at the burrow almost casually. I dived for it, scrambled into a damp chill and an odor as solid as well-aged cheese. A crawl of five feet brought me to a drop-off. I felt around over the edge, found the floor two feet below, swung my legs around and stood, facing the entrance with the slug gun in my hand. If Big Boy came in after me, he'd get a surprise.

But I saw the two of them silhouetted against the light from along the corridor. Lefty was leaning on his friend, making plaintive squeaking noises. Then they went off along the corridor together. Apparently whatever their instructions were, they didn't include taking revenge on the new specimen—not yet.

CHAPTER FOUR

The traditional first move when imprisoned in the dark was to pace off the dimensions of the cell, a gambit which presumably lends a mystic sense of mastery over one's environment. Of course, I wasn't actually imprisoned. I could crawl back out into the corridor—but since I would undoubtedly meet Lefty before I had gone far, the idea lacked appeal. That left me with the pacing off to do.

I started from the opening, took a step which I estimated at three feet, and slammed against a wall. No help there.

Back at my starting point, I took a more cautious step, then another—

There was a sound from the darkness ahead. I stood, one foot poised, not breathing, listening. . . .

"*Vansi pa' me' zen pa'*," a mellow tenor voice said from the darkness. "*Sta' zi?*"

I backed a step. The gun was still in my hand. The other fellow had the advantage; his eyes would be used to the dark, and I was outlined against the faint glow from the tunnel. At the thought, I dropped flat, felt the cold wetness of the rough floor come through my clothes.

"*Bo'jou', ami,*" the voice said. "*E' vou Gallice?*"

Whoever he was, he was presumably a fellow prisoner. And the language he had spoken didn't sound much like the grunts and clicks of the ogres outside. Still, I had no impulse to rush over and get acquainted.

"*Kansh' tu dall' Scansk . . .*" the voice came again. And this time I almost got the meaning. The accent was horrible, but it sounded almost like Swedish. . . .

"Maybe Anglic, you," the voice said.

"Maybe," I answered, hearing my voice come out as a croak. "Who're you?"

"Ah, good! I took a blink from you so you come into." The accent was vaguely Hungarian and the words didn't make much sense. "Why catch they you? Where from commer you?"

I edged a few feet to the side to get farther from the light. The floor slanted up slightly. I thought of using my lighter, but that would only make me a better target if this new chum had any unfriendly ideas—and nothing I had encountered so far in giant-land led me to expect otherwise.

"Don't be shy of you," the voice urged. "I am friend."

"I asked you who you are," I said. My hackles were still on edge. I was tired and hungry and bruised, and talking to a strange voice in the dark wasn't what I needed to soothe my nerves just now.

"Sir, I have honor of to make known myself: Field Agent Dzok, at the service."

"Field agent of what?" My voice had a sharp edge.

"Perhaps better for further confidences to await closer acquaintance," the field agent said. "Please, you will talk again, thus allowing me to place the dialect more closely."

"The dialect is English," I said. I eased back another foot, working my way up-slope. I didn't know whether he could see me or not, but it was an old maxim to take the high ground. . . .

"English? Ah, yes. I think we've triggered the correct mnemonic now. Not a very well-known sub-branch of Anglic, but then I fancy my linguistic indoctrination is one of the more complete for an Agent of Class Four. Am I doing better?"

The voice seemed closer, as well as more grammatical. "You're doing fine," I assured it—and rolled quickly away. Too late, I felt an edge under my back, yelled, went over, and slammed against hard stone three feet below the upper level. I felt my head bounce, heard a loud ringing, while bright lights flashed. Then there was a hand groping over my chest, under my head.

"Sorry, old fellow," the voice said up close. "I should have warned you. Did the same thing myself my first day here. . . ."

I sat up, groped quickly, found the slug gun, tucked it back into my cuff holster.

"I guess I was a little over-cautious," I said. "I hardly expected to run into another human being in this damned place." I worked my jaw, found it still operable, touched a scrape on my elbow.

"I see you've hurt your arm," my cell-mate said. "Let me dab a bit of salve on that. . . ." I heard him moving, heard the snap of some sort of fastener, fumbling noises. I got out my lighter, snapped it. It caught, blazed up blindingly. I held it up—and my jaw dropped.

Agent Dzok crouched a yard from me, his head turned away from the bright light, a small first aid kit in his hands— hands that were tufted with short, silky red-brown hair that ran up under the grimy cuffs of a tattered white uniform. I saw long thick-looking arms, scuffed soft leather boots encasing odd long-heeled feet, a small round head, dark-skinned, long nosed. Dzok turned his face toward me, blinking deepset yellowish eyes set close together above a wide mouth that opened in a smile to show square, yellow teeth.

"The light's a bit bright," he said in his musical voice. "I've been in the dark for so long now. . . . "

31

I gulped, flicked off the lighter. "Sorry," I mumbled. "Wha—who did you say you were?"

"You look a trifle startled," Dzok said in an amused tone. "I take it you haven't encountered my branch of the Hominids before?"

"I had a strange idea we Homo sapiens were the only branch of the family that made it into the Cenozoic," I said. "Meeting the boys outside was quite a shock. Now you. . . ."

"Ummm. I think our two families diverged at about your late Pliocene. The Hagroon are a somewhat later offshoot, at about the end of the Pleistocene—say half a million years back." He laughed softly. "So you see, they represent a closer relationship to you sapiens than do we of Xonijeel. . . ."

"That's depressing news."

Dzok's rough-skinned hand fumbled at my arm, then gripped it lightly while he dabbed at the abrasion. The cool ointment started to take the throb from the wound.

"How did they happen to pick you up?" Dzok asked. "I take it you were one of a group taken on a raid?"

"As far as I know, I'm the only one." I was still being cautious. Dzok seemed like a friendly enough creature, but he had a little too much hair on him for my taste, in view of what I'd seen of the Hagroon. The latter might be closer relatives of mine than of the agent, but I couldn't help lumping them together in my mind—though Dzok was more monkey-like than ape-like.

"Curious," Dzok said. "The pattern usually calls for catches of at least fifty or so. I've theorized that this represents some sort of minimum group size which is worth the bother of the necessary cultural analysis, language indoctrination, and so on."

"Necessary for what?"

"For making use of the captives," Dzok said. "The Hagroon are slave raiders, of course."

"Why 'of course'?"

"I assumed you knew, being a victim . . ." Dzok paused. "But then perhaps you're in a different category. You say you were the only captive taken?"

"What about you?" I ignored the question. "How did you get here?"

The agent sighed. "I was a trifle incautious, I fear. I had a rather naïve idea that in this congeries of variant hominid strains I'd pass unnoticed, but I was spotted instantly. They knocked me about a bit, dragged me in before a tribunal of nonagenarians for an interrogation, which I pretended not to understand—"

"You mean you speak their language?" I interrupted.

"Naturally, my dear fellow. An agent of Class Four could hardly be effective without language indoctrination."

I let that pass. "What sort of questions did they ask you?"

"Lot of blooming nonsense, actually. It's extremely difficult for noncosmopolitan races to communicate at a meaningful level; the basic cultural assumptions vary so widely—"

"You and I seem to be doing all right."

"Well, after all, I *am* a Field Agent of the Authority. We're trained in just such communicative ability."

"Maybe you'd better start a little farther back. What authority are you talking about? How'd you get here? Where are you from in the first place? Where did you learn English?"

Dzok had finished with my arm now. He laughed—a good-natured chuckle. Imprisonment in foul conditions seemed not to bother him. "I'll take those questions one at a time. I suggest we move up to my dais now. I've arranged a few scraps of cloth in the one dry corner here. And perhaps you'd like a bit of clean food, after that nauseous pap our friends here issue."

"You've got food?"

"My emergency ration pack. I've been using it sparingly. Not very satisfying, but nourishing enough."

We made our way to a shelf-like flat area high in the right rear corner of the cell, and I stretched out on Dzok's neatly arranged dry rags and accepted a robin's-egg-sized capsule.

"Swallow that down," Dzok said. "A balanced ration for twenty-fours hours; arranged concentrically, of course. Takes about nine hours to assimilate. There's water too." He passed me a thick clay cup.

I gulped hard, got the pill down. "Your throat must be bigger than mine," I said. "Now what about my questions?"

"Ah, yes, the Authority; this is the great Web government which exercises jurisdiction over all that region of the Web lying within two million E-units radius of the Home Line. . . ."

I was listening, thinking how this news would sit with the Imperial authorities when I got back—if I got back—if there was anything to go back to. Not one new Net-traveling race but two—each as alien to the other as either was to me. And all three doubtless laying claim to ever-wider territory. . . .

Dzok was still talking, ". . . our work in the Anglic sector has been limited, for obvious reasons—"

"What obvious reasons?"

"Our chaps could hardly pass unnoticed among you," Dzok said drily. "So we've left the sector pretty much to its own devices—"

"But you *have* been there?"

"Routine surveillance only, mostly in null time, of course—"

"You use too many 'of courses', Dzok," I said. "But go on, I'm listening."

"Our maps of the area are sketchy. There's the vast desert area, of C—" he cleared his throat. "A vast desert area known as the Desolation, within which no world lines survive, surrounded by a rather wide spectrum of related lines, all having as their central cultural source the North European technical nucleus—rather a low-grade technology, to be sure, but the first glimmering of enlightenment is coming into being there. . . ."

He went on with his outline of the vast sweep of A-lines that constituted the scope of activities of the Authority. I didn't call attention to his misconceptions regarding the total absence of life in the Blight, or his seeming ignorance of the existence of a line with Net-traveling capabilities. That was information I would keep in reserve.

". . . the scope of the Authority has been steadily extended over the last fifteen hundred years," the agent was saying. "Our unique Web-transit abilities naturally carry with them a certain responsibility. The early tendency toward exploitation has long been overcome, and the Authority now merely exercises a police and peace-keeping function, while obtaining useful raw materials and manufactured products from carefully selected loci on a normal commercial basis."

"Uh-huh." I'd heard the speech before. It was a lot like the pitch Bernadotte and Richthofen and the others had given me when I first arrived at Stockholm Zero-zero.

"My mission here," Dzok went on, "was to discover the forces behind the slave raids which had been creating so much misery and unrest along the periphery of the Authority, and to recommend the optimum method for eliminating the nuisance with the minimum of overt interference. As I've told you, I badly underestimated our Hagroon. I was arrested within a quarter-hour of my arrival."

"And you learned English on your visits to the, ah, Anglic Sector?"

"I've never visited the sector personally, but the language

34

libraries naturally have monitored the developing dialects."

"Do your friends know where you are?"

Dzok sighed. "I'm afraid not. I was out to cut a bit of a figure, I realize now—belatedly. I envisioned myself reporting back in to IDMS Headquarters with the solution neatly wrapped and tied with pink ribbon. Instead—well, in time they'll notice my prolonged absence and set to work to find my trail. In the meantime . . ."

"In the meantime, what?"

"I can only hope they take action before my turn comes."

"Your turn for what?"

"Didn't you know, old chap? But of course not; you don't speak their beastly dialect. It's all because of the food shortage, you see. They're cannibals. Captives that fail to prove their usefulness as slaves are slaughtered and eaten."

"About how long," I asked Dzok, "do you suppose we have?"

"I estimate that I've been here for three weeks," the agent said. "There were two poor sods here when I came—a pair of slaves of a low order of intelligence. As well as I could determine, they'd been here for some two weeks. They were taken away a week ago. Some sort of feast for a high official, I gathered. Judging from the look of the menu, they'd have need of those ferocious teeth of theirs. Tough chewing, I'd say."

I was beginning to see through agent Dzok. His breezy air covered a conviction that he'd be in a Hagroon cooking pot himself before many more days had passed.

"In that case, I suppose we'd better start thinking about a way to get out of here," I suggested.

"I hoped you'd see that," Dzok said. "I have a scheme of sorts—but it will require two men. How good are you at climbing?"

"As good as I have to be," I said shortly. "What's the plan?"

"There are two guards posted along the corridor. We'll need to entice one of them inside so as to deal with him separately. That shouldn't be too difficult."

"How do we get past the other one?"

"That part's a bit tricky—but not impossible. I have some materials tucked away here—items from my survival kit as well as number of things I've salvaged since I arrived. There's also a crude map I sketched from memory. We'll have approximately one hundred meters of corridor to negotiate be-

35

fore we reach the side entry I've marked as our escape route. Our only hope lies in not running into a party of Hagroon before we reach it. Your disguise won't stand close examination."

"Disguise?" I had the feeling I had stumbled into somebody else's drunken dream. "Who are we going as? Dracula and the wolf man?" I was light-headed, dizzy. I lay back on my rags and closed my eyes. Dzok's voice seemed to come from a long way off:

"Get a good rest. I'll make my preparations. As soon as you wake, we'll make our try."

I came awake to the sound of voices—snarling, angry voices. I sat up, blinking through deep gloom. Dzok said something in a mild tone, and the voice snapped back—a booming, animal snort. I could smell him now—even in the fetid air of the cell, the reek of the angry Hagroon cut through. I could see him, a big fellow, standing near the entry. I wondered how he'd gotten through; the opening was barely big enough for me. . . .

"Lie still and make no sound, Anglic," Dzok called in the same soothing tone he had been using to the Hagroon. "This one wants me. My time ran out, it seems. . . ." Then he broke into the strange dialect again.

The Hagroon snarled and spat. I saw his arm reach, saw Dzok duck under it, plant a solid blow in the bigger creature's chest. The Hagroon grunted, crouched a little, reached again. I came to my feet, flicked my wrist, felt the solid slap as the slug gun filled my palm. Dzok moved back and the jailor jumped after him, swung a blow that knocked the agent's guard aside and sent him spinning. I took two quick steps to the Hagroon's side, aimed, and fired at point-blank range. The recoil kicked me halfway across the room as the monster-man reeled back, fell to the floor, kicking, his long arms wrapped around himself. He was making horrible, choked sounds, and I felt myself pitying the brute. He was tough. The blast from the slug at that range would have killed an ox, but he was rolling over now, trying to get up. I followed him, picked out his head against the lesser dark of the background, fired again. Fluid spattered my face. The huge body gave one tremendous leap and lay still. I wiped my face with a forearm, snorted the rusty odor of blood from my nostrils, turned back to Dzok. He was sprawled on the floor, holding one arm.

"You fooled me, Anglic," he panted. "Damned good show . . . you had a weapon. . . ."

"What about that plan?" I demanded. "Can we try it now?"

"Damned . . . brute," Dzok got out between his teeth. "Broke my arm. Damned nuisance. Perhaps you'd better try it alone."

"To hell with that. Let's get started. What do I do?"

Dzok made a choked sound that might have been a laugh. "You're tougher than you look, Anglic, and the gun will help. All right. Here's what we have to do . . ."

Twenty minutes later I was sweating inside the most fantastic getup ever used in a jail break. Dzok had draped me in a crude harness made from strips of rags—there had been a heap of them in the den when he arrived—luxurious bedding for the inmates. Attached to the straps were tufts of greasy hair arranged so as to hang down, screening my body. The agent had traded his food ration to his former cell-mates in return for the privilege of trimming hair samples from their shaggy bodies, he explained. The dead Hagroon had supplied more. Using adhesives from his kit, he had assembled the grotesque outfit. It hung down below my knees, without even an attempt at a fit.

"This is fantastic," I told him. "It wouldn't fool a newborn idiot at a hundred yards in a bad light!"

Agent Dzok was busy stuffing a bundle inside what was left of his jacket. "You'll look properly bulky and shaggy. That's the best we can do. You won't have to pass close scrutiny—we hope. Now let's be going."

Dzok went first, moving awkwardly with his broken arm bound to his chest, but not complaining. He paused with his head out in the corridor, then scrabbled through.

"Come on, the coast is clear," he called softly. "Our warden is taking a stroll."

I followed, emerged into air that was comparatively cool and clean after the stale stink of the den. The light was on along the passage as usual. There was no way to tell the time of day. A hundred feet along, the corridor turned right and up; there were no openings along the section we could see. The guard was presumably loitering farther along.

Dzok moved silently off, slim-hipped, low-waisted, his odd, thin legs slightly bent at the knee, his once natty uniform a thing of tatters and tears through which his seal-sleek pelt showed. Before we reached the turn, we heard the rumble of Hagroon voices. Dzok stopped and I came up beside him. He stood with his head cocked, listening.

"Two of them," he whispered. "Filthy bit of luck. . . ."

I waited feeling the sweat trickle down inside my clown suit of stinking rags and dangling locks of hair. There was a sudden sharp itch between my shoulder blades—not the first since I had been introduced to Hagroon hospitality. I grimaced but didn't try to scratch; the flimsy outfit would have fallen to pieces.

"Oh-oh," Dzok breathed. "One of them is leaving. Changing of the guard."

I nodded. Another minute ticked by like a waiting bomb. Dzok turned, gave me a large wink, then said something in a loud, angry snarl—a passable imitation of the Hagroon speech pattern. He waited a moment, then hissed: "Count to ten, slowly—" and started on along the passage at a quick, shambling pace. Just as he moved out of sight around the corner, he looked back, shouted something in a chattering language. Then he was gone.

I started my count, listening hard. I heard the Hagroon guard snort something, heard Dzok reply. Five. Six. Seven. The Hagroon spoke again, sounding closer. Nine. Ten—

I took a deep breath, tried to assume the sort of hunch-shouldered stance the Hagroon displayed, moved on around the turn in a rolling walk. Twenty feet ahead, beyond the light, Dzok stood, waving his good arm, yelling something now, pointing back toward me. A few yards farther on, the guard, a squat, bristly figure like a pile of hay, shot a glance in my direction. Dzok jumped closer to him, still shouting. The Hagroon raised an arm, took a swing that Dzok just managed to avoid. I came on, getting closer to the light bulb now. Dzok dashed, in, ducked, got past the guard. The Hagroon had his back to me, fifteen feet away now, almost within range. I flipped the gun into my hand, made another five feet—

The guard whirled, started an angry shout at me—then suddenly got a good look at what must have been only a dim silhouette in the bad light at his first glance. His reflexes were good. He lunged while the startled look was still settling into place on the wide, mud-colored face. I got the shot off just as he crashed into me, and we went down, his four-hundred-pound body smashing me back like a truck hitting a fruit cart. I managed to twist aside just enough to let the bulk of his weight slam past before I hit the pavement and skidded. I got some breath back into my lungs, hauled my gun hand free for another shot. But it wasn't necessary—the huge body lay sprawled half on me, inert as a frozen mammoth.

Dzok was beside me, helping me to my feet with his good hand.

"All right, so far," he said cheerfully rearranging my hair shirt. "Quite a weapon you have there. You sapiens are marvelous at that sort of thing—a natural result of your physical frailty, no doubt."

"Let's analyze me later," I muttered. My shoulders were hurting like hell where I had raked them across the rough paving. "What next?"

"Nothing else between us and the refuse disposal slot I told you about. It's not far. Come along." He seemed as jaunty as ever, unbothered by the brief, violent encounter.

He led the way down a slanting side branch, then up a steep climb, took another turnoff into a wider passage filled with the smell of burning garbage.

"The kitchens," Dzok hissed. "Just a little farther."

We heard loud voices then—the Hagroon never seemed to talk any other way. Flat against the rough-hewn wall, we waited. Two slope-shouldered bruisers waddled out from the low-arched kitchen entry, and went off in the opposite direction. We went on, following a trail of spilled refuse, ducked under a low doorway and into a bin layered with putrefying food waste. I thought I had graduated from the course in bad smells, but this was a whole new spectrum of stench. We splashed through, looked out a two-yard-wide, foot-high slot crusted with garbage. The view was darkness, and a faint glistening of wet cobbles far below. I twisted, looked up. A ragged line of eaves showed above my head.

"I thought so," I said softly. "The low ceilings meant the roof had to be next. I think these people stacked this pile of stone up here and carved the rooms out afterward."

"Precisely," Dzok said. "Not very efficient, perhaps, but in a society where slave labor is plentiful and architectural talent nonexistent, it serves."

"Which way?" I asked. "Up or down?"

Dzok looked doubtfully at me, eyeing my shoulders and arms like a fight manager looking over a prospective addition to his stable. "Up," he said. "If you think you can manage."

"I guess I'll have to manage," I said. "And what about you, with that arm?"

"Eh? Oh, it may be a bit awkward, but no matter. Shall we go?" And he slipped forward through the opening in the two-foot thick wall, twisting over on his back; then his feet were through and out of sight, and suddenly I was very much alone. Behind me the growl of voices and an occasional clatter seemed louder than it had before. Someone was coming my way. I turned over on my back as Dzok had done, eased into the slot. The garbage provided adequate lubrication.

My head emerged into the chilly night. Above I saw the cold glitter of stars in a pitch-black sky, the dim outlines of nearby buildings, a few faint lights gleaming from openings cut at random in the crude masonry walls. It was a long reach to the projecting cornice just above me. I stretched, trying not to think about the long drop below—found a handhold, scrambled up and over. Dzok came up, as I rolled and sat up.

"There's a bridge to the next tower a few yards down the far side," he whispered. "What kept you?"

"I just paused to admire the view. Here, help me get rid of the ape suit." I shed the costume, caked and slimy with garbage now, while Dzok slapped ineffectually at the samples adhering to my back. He looked worse than I did, if possible. His sleek fur was damp and clotted with sour-smelling liquid.

"When I get home," he said, "I shall have the longest, hottest bath obtainable in the most luxurious sensorium in the city of Zaj."

"I'll join you there," I offered. "If we make it."

"The sooner we start, the sooner the handmaidens will ply their brushes." He moved away across the slight dome of the roof, crouched at the far edge, turned, and slipped from sight. It appeared that there was a lot more monkey in Dzok than I'd managed to retain. I got down awkwardly on all fours, slid over the edge, groped with a foot, found no support.

"Lower yourself to arm's length," Dzok's voice came softly from the darkness below—how far below I couldn't say. I eased over the edge, scraping new abrasions in my hide. Dangling at full length, I still found nothing under my toes.

"Let go and drop," Dzok called quietly. "Just a meter or so."

That was a proposal I would have liked to mull over in the quiet of my study for a few hours, but it wasn't the time to argue. I tried to relax, then let go. There was a dizzy moment of free fall, a projecting stone ripped my cheek as I slammed against a flat ledge and went down, one hand raking stone, the other stabbing down into nothingness. Dzok caught me, pulled me back. I sat up, made out the dim strip of dark, rail-less walk arching off into the night. I started to ask if that was what we had to cross, but Dzok was already on the way.

Forty-five minutes later, after a trip that would have been unexceptional to the average human fly, Dzok and I stood in the deep shadow of an alley carpeted in the usual deposit of rubbish.

"This place would be an archaeologist's paradise," I muttered. "Everything from yesterday's banana peel to the first fling they ever chipped is right here underfoot."

Dzok was busy opening the bundle he had carried inside his jacket. I helped him arrange the straps and brasses taken from the Hagroon I had killed in the cell.

"We'll exchange roles now," he said softly. "I'm the captor, if anyone questions us. I may be able to carry it off. I'm not certain just how alien I may appear to the average monster in the street; I saw a few australopithecine types as they brought me in. Now, it's up to you to guide us to where you left the shuttle. About half a mile, you said?"

"Something like that—if it's still there." We started off along the alley which paralleled the main thoroughfare I had traversed under guard eighteen hours earlier. It twisted and turned, narrowing at times to no more than an air space between crooked walls, widening once to form a marketplace where odd, three-tiered stalls slumped, deserted and drab in the postmidnight stillness. After half an hour's stealthy walk, I called a halt.

"The way these alleys wander, I'm not a damned bit sure where we are," I said. "I think we'll have to risk trying the main street, at least long enough for me to get my bearings."

Dzok nodded, and we took a side alley, emerging in the comparatively wide avenue. A lone Hagroon shambled along the opposite side of the street. Wide-spaced lamps on ten-foot poles shed pools of sad, yellow light on a littered walk that ran under windowless façades adorned only by the crooked lines of haphazard masonry courses, as alien as beehives.

I led the way to the right. A trough of brownish stone slopping over with oil-scummed water looked familiar; just beyond this point I had seen the harnessed mastodon. The alley from which the shuttle had operated was not far ahead. The street curved to the left. I pointed to a dark side way debouching from a widening of the street ahead.

"I think that's it. We'd better try another alley and see if we can't sneak up on it from behind. They probably have guards on the shuttle."

"We'll soon know." A narrow opening just ahead seemed to lead back into the heart of the block of masonry. We

41

followed it, emerged in a dead end, from which an arched opening like a sewage tunnel led off into utter darkness.

"Let's try that route," Dzok suggested. "It seems to lead in the right general direction."

"What if it's somebody's bedroom?" I eyed the looming building; the crudely mortared walls gave no hint of interior function. The Hagroon knew only one style of construction: solid-rock Gothic.

"In that case, we'll beat a hasty retreat."

"Somehow the thought of pounding through these dark alleys with a horde of aroused Hagroon at my heels lacks appeal," I said. "But I guess we can give it a try." I moved to the archway, peered inside, then took the plunge. My shoes seemed loud on the rough floor. Behind me I could hear Dzok's breathing. The last glimmer of light faded behind us. I was feeling my way with a hand against the wall now. We went on for what seemed a long time.

"Hssst!" Dzok's hand touched my shoulder. "I think we've taken a wrong turning somewhere, old boy . . ."

"Yeah . . ." I thought it over. "We'd better go back."

For another ten minutes we groped our way back in the dark, as silently as possible. Then Dzok halted. I came up behind him.

"What is it?" I whispered.

"Shhh."

I heard it then: a very faint sound of feet shuffling. Then a glow of light sprang up around a curve ahead, showing a dark doorway across the passage.

"In there," Dzok whispered, and dived for it. I followed, slammed against him. There was a sound of heavy breathing nearby.

"What was that you said about bedrooms?" he murmured in my ear.

The breathing snorted into a resonant snore, followed by gulping sounds. I could hear a heavy body moving, the rustle of disturbed rubbish. Then an eerie silence settled.

Suddenly Dzok moved. I heard something clatter in the far corner of the room. His hand grabbed at me, pulling me along. I stumbled over things, heard his hand rasping on stone, then we were flat against the wall. A big Hagroon body rose up, moved into the light from the open door through which we had entered. Another of the shaggy figures appeared outside; this would be the one we had first heard in the alley. The two exchanged guttural growls. The nearer one turned back into the room—and abruptly the chamber was flooded with wan light. I saw that Dzok and I were in an alcove that partly concealed us from view from the door. The Hagroon squinted against the light, half-turned away—then whirled back as he saw us. Dzok jumped. The gun slapped my hand— but Dzok was past him, diving for another opening. I was behind him, ducking under the Hagroon's belated grab, then pelting along a tunnel toward a faint glow at the far end, Dzok bounding ten yards in the lead. There were yells behind us, a horrible barking roar, the pound of feet. I hadn't wanted a horde of trolls chasing me through the dark—but here I was anyway.

Ahead, Dzok leaped out into the open, skidded to a halt, looked both ways, then pointed, and was gone. I raced out into the open alley, saw Dzok charging straight at a pair of Hagroon in guards' bangles—and beyond him, the dark rectangular bulk of the shuttle. The agent yelled. I recognized the grunts and croaks of the Hagroon language. The two guards hesitated. One pointed at me, started forward, the other spread his arms, barked something at Dzok. The latter, still coming on full tilt, straight-armed the heavier humanoid, dodged aside as the Hagroon staggered back, and made for the shuttle. I brought the slug gun up, fired at extreme range, saw the Hagroon bounce back, slam against the wall, then reach—but I was past him. Dzok's opponent saw me, dithered for a moment, then whirled toward me. I fired—and missed, tried to twist aside, slipped, went down and skidded under the Hagroon's grasp, leaving a sleeve from my coat dangling in his hands. I scrambled, made it to all fours, dived for the open entry to the shuttle. Dzok's hand shot out, hauled me inside, and the door banged behind me as the sentry hit it like a charging rhino.

Dzok whirled to the operator's seat.

"Great Scott!" he yelled. "The control lever's broken off short!" The shuttle was rocking under blows at the entry port. Dzok gripped the edge of the panel with his one good hand; the muscles of his shoulder bunched, and with one heave, he tore it away, exposing tight-packed electronic components.

"Quick, Anglic!" he snapped. "The leads there—cross them!" I wedged myself in beside him, grabbed two heavy insulated cables, twisted their ends together. Following the agent's barked instructions, I ripped wires loose, made hasty connections from a massive coil—which I recognized as an M-C field energizer—to a boxed unit like a fifty KW trans-

43

former. Dzok reached past me, jammed a frayed cable end against a heavy bus bar. With a shower of blue and yellow sparks, copper welded to steel. A deep hum started up; abruptly the shattering blows at the entry ceased. I felt the familiar tension of the M-C field close in around me. I let out a long sigh, slumped back in the chair.

"Close, Anglic," Dzok sighed, "But we're clear now. . . ." I looked over at him, saw his yellowish eyes waver and half-close; then he fell sideways into my lap.

CHAPTER FIVE

Dzok was lying where I had dragged him, in deep grass under a small, leafy tree, his chest rising and falling in the quick, shallow, almost panting, breathing of his kind.

The shuttle rested fifty feet away, up against a rocky escarpment at the top of which a grey, chimp-sized ape perched, scratching thoughtfully amd gazing down at us. My clothes were spread on the grass along with what remained of Dzok's whites. I had given them a scrubbing in the sandy-bedded stream that flowed nearby. I had also inventoried my wounds, found nothing worse than cuts, scrapes and bruises.

The agent rolled over on his side, groaned, winced in his sleep as his weight pressed against his bound arm; then his eyes opened.

"Welcome back," I said. "Feel better?"

He groaned again. His pale tongue came out, touched his thin, blackish lips.

"As soon as I'm home again I shall definitely resign my commission," he croaked. He moved to ease the arm, lifted it with his good hand and laid it across his chest.

"This member seems to belong to someone else," he groaned. "Someone who died horribly."

"Maybe I'd better try to set it."

He shook his head. "Where are we, Anglic?"

"The name's Bayard. As to where we are, your guess is better than mine, I hope. I piled the scout along full tilt for about five hours, then took a chance and dropped in here to wait for you to come around. You must have been in worse shape than you told me."

"I was close to the end of my resources," the agent admitted. "I'd been beaten pretty badly on three occasions, and my

44

food pellets were running low. I'd been on short rations for about a week."

"How the devil did you manage to stay on your feet—and climb, and fight, and run—and with a broken arm?"

"Small credit to me, old fellow. Merely a matter of triggering certain emergency metabolic stimulators. Hypnotics, you know." His eyes took in the scene. "Pretty place. No sign of our former hosts?"

"Not yet. It's been about four hours since we arrived."

"I think we're safe from intrusion. From what little we'd learned of them, they have very poor Web instrumentation. They won't trail us." He studied the ragged skyline.

"Did you maneuver the shuttle spatially? We seem to be out in the wilds."

I shook my head. "These cliffs here," I indicated the rising pinnacles of warm, reddish-brown stone that ringed the glade. "I watched them evolve from what were buildings back in the inhabited regions. It gives you the feeling that we men and our works are just a force of nature, like any other catastrophe."

"I've seen the same thing," Dzok agreed. "No matter what path you choose to follow across the alternate world-lines, the changes are progressive, developmental. A puddle becomes a pond, then a lake, then a reservoir, then a swimming pool, then a swamp filled with dead trees and twenty-foot snakes; trees stretch, or shrink, grow new branches, new fruits, slide away through the soil to new positions; but always gradually. There are no discontinuities in the entropic grid—excepting, of course, such man-caused anomalies as the Desolation."

"Do you know where we are?" The grey ape on the cliff top watched me suspiciously.

"Give me a moment to gather my forces," Dzok closed his eyes, took deep breaths. "I'll have to drop back on self-hypnotic mnemonic conditioning. I have no conscious recollection of this region."

I waited. His breathing resumed its normal rapid, shallow pattern. His eyes popped open.

"Right," he said briskly. "Not too bad, at all. We're about six hours' run from Authority Central at Zaj, I'd guess." He sat up, got shakily to his feet. "May as well get moving. I'll have a bit of work to do calibrating the instruments; bit awkward navigating with dead screens." He was looking at me thoughtfully. "Which brings me to wonder, Bayard, ah ... just how did you manage to control the shuttle?"

45

I could feel my forehead wrinkling. I couldn't tell yet whether I was going to frown or grin.

"I may as well confide in you, Dzok," I said. "I know a little something about shuttles myself."

He waited, looking alert and interested.

"Your Authority isn't the only power claiming control of the Net. I represent the Paramount Government of the Imperium."

Dzok nodded kindly. "Glad you decided to tell me. Makes things cosier all around. Lends an air of mutual confidence, all that sort of thing."

"You already knew?'

"I must confess I used a simple hypnotic technique on you while you were resting, back in our digs. Dug out some fascinating data. Took the opportunity to plant a number of suggestions, too. Nothing harmful, of course. Just a little dampening of your anxiety syndrome, plus, of course, a command to obey my instructions to the letter."

I looked at him, gazing airily at me. My expression settled into a wide and rather sardonic grin.

"I'm very relieved to hear it. Now I don't feel like such a stinker for working on you while you were out."

For a moment he looked startled, then his complacent expression returned.

"Sorry to disappoint you, old chap, but of course I'm well protected against that sort of thing—" he broke off, looking just a little worried, as though a thought had just struck him.

I nodded. "Me too."

Suddenly he laughed. His cannonball head seemed to split in a grin that showed at least thirty-six teeth. He leaned and slapped his knee with his good hand, doubled over in a paroxysm of hilarity, staggered toward me, still roaring. I took a step back, tensed my wrist.

"You have an infectious laugh, Dzok," I said. "But not infectious enough to let you get me in range of that pile driver arm of yours."

He straightened, grinning rather ruefully now. "Seems to be a bit of an impasse," he conceded.

"I'm sure we can work it out," I said. "Just don't keep trying those beginners' tricks. I've had to learn all about them."

He pursed his wide, thin lips. "I'm wondering why you stopped here. Why didn't you press on, reattain the safety of your own base while I was unconscious?"

46

"I told you. I don't know where I am. This is unfamiliar territory to me—and there are no maps aboard that tub."

"Ah-hah. And now you expect me to guide you home—and myself into an untenable position?"

"Just rig up the board and calibrate it. I'll do my own steering."

He shook his head. "I'm still considerably stronger than you, old fellow—in spite of my indisposition." He twitched his broken arm. "I fail to see how you can coerce me."

"I still have the gun we sapiens are so clever about making."

"Quite. But shooting me would hardly be to your advantage." He was grinning again. I had the feeling he was enjoying it all. "Better let me run us in to Xonijeel. I'll see to it you're given all possible aid."

"I've had a sample of hairy hospitality," I said. "I'm not yearning for more."

He looked pained. "I hope you don't lump us australopithecines in with the Hagroon, of all people, just on the basis of a little handsome body hair."

"Are you promising me you'll give me a shuttle and turn me loose?"

"Well . . ." he spread his wide, deeply-grooved hands. "After all, I'm hardly in a position . . ."

"Think of the position you'd be in if I left you here."

"I'd have to actively resist any such effort, I'm afraid."

"You'd lose."

"Hmmm. Probably. On the other hand, I'd be much too valuable a prisoner in this Imperium of yours, so it's just as well to die fighting." He tensed as though ready to go into action. I didn't want that.

"I'll make another proposal," I said quickly. "You give me your word as an officer of the Authority that I'll be given an opportunity to confer with the appropriate high officials at Zaj—and I'll agree to accompany you there first."

He nodded promptly. "I can assure you of that much. And I'll take it upon myself to personally guarantee you'll receive honorable treatment."

"That's a deal." I stepped forward, put out my hand, trying not to look as worried as I felt. Dzok looked blank, then reached out gingerly, took my hand. His palm felt hot and dry and coarse-skinned, like a dog's paw.

"Empty hand; no weapon," he murmured. "Marvelous symbolism." He grinned widely again. "Glad we worked it

47

out. You seem like a decent sort, Bayard, in spite—" The smile faded slightly. "I have a curious feeling you've done me, in some obscure way. . . ."

"I was wondering how I'd talk you into taking me to Zaj," I said, grinning back at him now. "Thanks for making it easy."

"Ummm. Trouble at home, eh?"

"That's a slight understatement."

He frowned at me. I'll get to work on the instruments, while you tell me the details."

One hour, two skinned knuckles, and one slight electric shock later, the shuttle was on its way, Dzok in the operator's seat crouched over the jury-rigged panel.

"This curious light you mentioned," he was saying. "You say it seemed to pervade even enclosed spaces, cut off from any normal light source?"

"That's right. A sort of ghostly, bluish glow."

"There are a number of things in your account that I can't explain," Dzok said. "But as for the light effect, it's plain you'd been transposed spontaneously into a null-time level. The Hagroon are fond of operating there. The apparent light is due to certain emanations arising from the oscillation of elementary particles at a vastly reduced level of energy; a portion of this activity elicits a response from the optic nerve. Did you notice that it arose particularly from metal surfaces?"

"Not especially."

Dzok shook his head, frowning. "A fantastic energy input is required to transfer mass across the entropic threshold. Far more than is needed to set up the drift across the A-lines, for example. And you say you found yourself there, without mechanical aid?"

I nodded. "What is this null time?"

"Ah, a very difficult concept." Dzok was busily noting instrument readings, twiddling things, taking more readings. As a shuttle technician, he was way ahead of me. "In normal entropy, of course, we move in a direction which we can conveniently think of as forward; with Web travel, we move perpendicular to this vector—sideways, one might say. Null time . . . well, consider it as offset at right angles to both: a stunted, lifeless continuum, in which energies flow in strange ways."

"Then it wasn't the city that was altered—it was me. I had

48

been ejected from my normal continuum into this null-time state—"

"Quite correct, old fellow," Dzok blinked at me sympathetically. "I can see you've been laboring under a ghastly strain, thinking otherwise."

"I'm beginning to get the picture," I said. "The Hagroon are studying the Imperium from null time—getting set for an attack, I'd guess offhand. They've got techniques that are way beyond anything the Imperium has. We need help. Do you think the Authority will give it to us?"

"I don't know, Bayard," Dzok said. "But I'll do my best for you."

I had a few hours' restless nap on the floor behind the control seat before Dzok called me. I climbed up to lean over his chair, staring into the screen. We were among spidery towers now; minarets of lofty, fragile beauty, soaring up pink, yellow, pale green, into a bright morning sky.

"Nice," I said. "We're close to your home line now, I take it?"

"Ah, the towers of Zaj," Dzok almost sang. "There's nothing to equal them in all the universes!"

"Let's hope I get a reception to match the pretty buildings."

"Look here, Bayard, there's something I feel I ought to . . . ah . . . tell you," Dzok said hesitantly. "Frankly, there's a certain, well, ill-feeling in the minds of some against the sapiens group. Unreasonable, perhaps—but it's a factor we're going to have to deal with."

"What's this ill-feeling based on?"

"Certain, ah, presumed racial characteristics. You have a reputation for ferocity, ruthless competitiveness, love of violence. . . ."

"I see. We're not nice and mild like the Hagroon, say. And who was it that I saw bounce one of the Hagroon out of the way in order to steal this scout we're riding in?"

"Yes, yes, all of us are prey to a certain degree of combativeness. But perhaps you noticed that even the Hagroon tend to enslave rather than to kill, and though they're cruel, it's the cruelty of indifference, not hate. I saw you kick one of them just as you entered the cell. Did you note that he took no revenge?"

"Anybody will fight back when he's been knocked around enough."

"But only you sapiens have systematically killed off every other form of hominid life in your native continua!" Dzok was getting a little excited now. "You hairless ones—in every line where you exist—you exist alone! Ages ago, in the first confrontation of the bald mutation with normal anthropos— driven, doubtless, by shame at your naked condition—you slaughtered your hairy fellow men! And even today your minds are warped by ancient guilt-and-shame complexes associated with nudity!"

"So you're holding the present generation responsible for what happened—or may have happened—thousands of years ago?"

"In my world sector," Dzok stated, "there are three major races of Man: we australopithecines, to employ your English term; the Rhodesians—excellent workers, strong and willing, if not overly bright; and the Pekin derivatives—blue-faced chaps, you know. We live together in perfect harmony, each group with its societal niche, each contributing its special talents to the common culture. While you sapiens—why, you even set upon your own kind, distinguishable only by the most trivial details!"

"What about me, Dzok? Do I seem to you to be a raving maniac? Have I indicated any particular distaste for you, for example?"

"Me?" Dzok looked amazed, then whooped with laughter. "Me!" he choked. "The idea . . ."

"What's so funny?"

"You . . . with your poor bald face—your spindly limbs— your degenerate dentition—having to overcome your natural distaste for *me*!" He was almost falling out of his chair now.

"Well, if I had any natural distaste, I at least had the decency to forget it!" I snapped.

Dzok stopped laughing, dabbed at his eyes with a dangling cuff. He looked at me almost apologetically.

"You did, at that," he conceded. "And you bound up my arm, and washed my poor old uniform for me—"

"And your poor old face too, you homely galoot!"

Dzok was smiling embarrassedly now. "I'm sorry, old boy; I got a bit carried away. All those personal remarks—a lot of rot, actually. Judge a chap on what he does, not what he is, eh? None of us can help our natural tendencies—and perhaps overcoming one's instinct is in the end a nobler achievement than not having the impulse in the first place." He put out his hand uncertainly.

"Empty hand, no weapon, eh?" He smiled. I took the hand.

"You're all right, Bayard," Dzok said. "Without you I'd have been rotting in that bloody cell. I'm on your side, old fellow—all the way!"

He whirled as a buzzer went, slapped switches, threw out the main drive, watched needles creep across dials, flipped the transfer switch. The growl of the field generators faded down the scale. Dzok beamed at me.

"We're here." He held a thumb up. "This may be a great day for both our races."

We stepped out into a wide sweep of colorfully tiled plaza dotted with trees, the bright geometric shapes of flower beds, fountains splashing in the sunlight. There were hundreds of australopithecines in sight, strolling leisurely in pairs, or hurrying briskly along with the air of urgency that was apparently as characteristic of Xonijeelian bureaucrats as of their hairless counterparts at home. Some wore flowing robes like Arab djellabas; others were dressed in multicolored pantaloon and jacket outfits; and here and there were the trim white uniforms that indicated the IDMS. Our sudden arrival in the midst of the pack caused a mild stir that became a low murmur as they caught sight of me. I saw noses wrinkle in flat, toothy faces, a few hostile stares, heard snickers from here and there. Someone called something to Dzok. He answered, took a firm grip on my arm.

"Sorry, Bayard," he muttered. "Mustn't appear to be running loose, you know." He waved an arm at a light aircraft cruising overhead. I thought it was a heli until I noticed its lack of rotors. It dropped into a landing and a wide transparent hatch opened like a clamshell. A close relative of Dzok's showed a fine set of teeth and waved, then his gaze settled on me and his grin dropped like a wet bar rag. He fluted something at Dzok, who called an answer back, took my arm, urged me along.

"Ignore him, Bayard. A mere peasant."

"That's easy. I don't know what he's saying."

I climbed into the well-sprung seat. Dzok settled in beside me, gave the driver an address.

"This adventure hasn't turned out too badly after all," he said expansively. "Back safe and sound—more or less—with a captive machine and a most unusual, ah, guest."

"I'm glad you didn't say prisoner," I commented, looking down on a gorgeous pattern of parks and plazas and delicate spires as we swooped over them at dashing speed. "Where are we headed?"

"We're going directly to IDMS Headquarters. My report will require quick action, and of course you're in haste as well."

There didn't seem to be much more to say. I rode along, admiring the city below, watching a massive white tower grow in the distance. We aimed directly for it, circled it once as though waiting for landing instructions, then hovered, dropped down to settle lightly on a small pad centered in a roof garden of tall palms, great banks of yellow and blue blossoms, free-form reflecting pools, with caged birds and animals completing the jungle setting.

"Now, just let me do the talking, Bayard," Dzok said, hurrying me toward a stairwell. "I'll present your case to our Council in the most favorable light, and I'm confident there'll be no trouble. You should be on your way home in a matter of hours."

"I hope your Council is a little less race-minded than the yokels down below——" I started, then broke off, staring at a camouflaged cage where a hairless, tailless biped, two-feet tall, with a low forehead, snouted face and sparse beard stared out at me with dull eyes.

"My God!" I said. "That's a man—a midget——"

Dzok turned sharply. "Eh? What?" He gaped, then grinned. "Oh, good Lord, Bayard, it's merely a tonquil! Most amusing little creature, but hardly human——"

The little manikin stirred, made a plaintive noise. I went on then, feeling a mixture of emotions, none of which added to my confidence.

We descended the escalator, went along a wide, cool corridor to a glass door, on into a wide skylighted room with a pool, grass, tables, and a row of lockers at the far side. Dzok went to a wall screen, talked urgently, then turned to me.

"All set," he told me. "Council's in session now, and will review the case."

"That's fast action," I said. "I was afraid I'd have to spend a week filling out forms and then sweat out a spot on the calendar."

"Not here," Dzok said loftily. "It's a matter of pride for local Councils to keep their dockets clear."

"Local Council? I thought we were going to see the big wheels. I need to make my pitch to the top level——"

"This is the top level. They're perfectly capable of evaluat-

52

ing a situation, making a sound decision, and issuing appropriate orders." He glanced at a wall scale which I assumed was a clock.

"We have half an hour. We'll take a few moments to freshen up, change of clothes and all that. I'm afraid we still smell of the Hagroon prison."

There were a few other customers in the room, lanky, sleek Xonijeelians who stroked to the length of the pool or reclined in lounge chairs. They stared curiously as we passed. Dzok spoke to one or two, but didn't linger to chat. At the lockers, he pressed buttons, used an attached tape to measure me, worked a lever. A flat package popped out from a wide slot.

"A clean outfit, Bayard—not exactly what you've been used to, but I think you'll find it comfortable—and frankly, the familiar garments may be a help in overcoming any initial—ah—distaste the Council Members may feel."

"Swell," I muttered. "Too bad I left my ape suit. I could come as a Hagroon."

Dzok tutted and selected clothing for himself, then led me into a shower room where jets of warm, perfumed water came from orifices in the domed ceiling. We stripped and soaped down, Dzok achieving a remarkable lather, then air-dried in the dressing room. My new clothes—a pantaloon and jacket outfit in blue and silver satin with soft leather-like shoes and white silk shirt—fitted me passably. Dzok snickered, watching me comb my hair. I think he considered it hardly worth the effort. He gave the mirror a last glance, settled his new gold-braided white pillbox cap on his round head, fitted the scarlet chin strap under his lower lip, gave the tight-fitting tunic a last tug. "Not often an agent returns from the field with a report he's justified in classifying Class Two Sub-Emergency," he said in a satisfied tone.

"What's the emergency? Me or the Hagroon slave-runners?"

Dzok laughed—a bit uneasily, perhaps. "Now, now, don't be anxious, Bayard. I'm sure the Councillors will recognize the unusual nature of your case...."

I followed him back into the corridor, thinking that one over.

"Suppose I were a 'usual' case, what then?"

"Well, of course, Authority policy would govern in that instance. But—"

"And what would Authority policy dictate?" I persisted.

"Let's just wait and deal with the situation as it develops,

53

eh?" Dzok hurried ahead, leaving me with an unpleasant feeling that his self-confidence was waning the closer we came to the huge red-gilt doors that blocked the wide corridor ahead.

Two sharp sentries in silver-trimmed white snapped to as we came up. Dzok exchanged a few words with them. Then one thumbed a control and the portals swung open. Dzok took a deep breath, waiting for me to come up. Beyond him I saw a long table behind which sat a row of faces—mostly australopithecines, but with representatives of at least three other types of Man, all with grey or grizzled heads, some in red-ornamented whites, a few in colorful civvies.

"Stiff upper lip, that's the drill," Dzok muttered. "To my left and half a pace back. Follow my lead on protocol. . . ." Then he stepped off toward the waiting elders. I adjusted a nonviolent, uncompetitive look on my face and followed. A dozen pairs of yellow eyes watched me approach; twelve expressions faced me across the polished table of black wood— and none of them were warm smiles of welcome. A narrow-faced grey-beard to the left of center made a smacking noise with his mobile lips, leaned to mutter something to the councillor on his left. Dzok halted, executed a half-bow with a bending of the knees, spoke briefly in his staccato language, then indicated me.

"I introduce to the Council one Bayard, native to the Anglic Sector," he said, switching to English. "As you see, a sapiens—"

"Where did you capture it?" the thin-faced member rapped out in a high, irritable voice.

"Bayard is not . . . ah . . . precisely a captive, Excellency," Dzok started.

"Are you saying the creature forced its way here?"

"You may ignore that question, Agent," a round-faced councillor spoke up from the right. "Councillor Sphogeel is venting his bias in rhetoric. However, your statement requires clarification."

"You're aware of Authority policy with regard to bald anthropoids, Agent?" another put in.

"The circumstances under which I encountered Bayard were unusual," Dzok said smoothly. "It was only with his cooperation and assistance that I escaped prolonged imprisonment. My report—"

"Imprisonment? An Agent of the Authority?"

"I think we'd better hear the Agent's full report—at once,"

the councillor who had interrupted Sphogeel said, then added a remark in Xonijeelian. Dzok replied in kind at some length, with considerable waving of his long arms. I stood silently at his left and a half pace to the rear as instructed, feeling like a second hand bargain up for sale, with no takers.

The councillors fired questions then, which Dzok fielded crisply, sweating all the while. Old Sphogeel's expression failed to sweeten as the hearing went on. Finally the round-faced councillor waved a long-fingered, greyish hand, fixed his gaze on me.

"Now, Bayard, Agent Dzok has told us of the circumstances under which you placed yourself in his custody——"

"I doubt very much that Dzok told you any such thing," I cut him off abruptly. "I'm here by invitation, as a representative of my government."

"Is the Council to be subjected to impertinence?" Sphogeel demanded shrilly. "You speak when ordered to do so, sapiens—and keep a civil tongue in your head!"

"And I'm also sure," I bored on, "that his report included mention of the fact that I'm in need of immediate transportation back to my home line."

"Your needs are hardly of interest to this body," Sphogeel snapped. "We know quite well how to deal with your kind."

"You don't know anything about my kind!" I came back at him. "There's been no previous contact between our respective governments——"

"There is only one government, sapiens!" Sphogeel cut me off. "As for your kind . . ." His long, flexible upper lip was curled back, showing shocking pink gums and lots of teeth, in a sneer like that of an annoyed horse. ". . . we're familiar enough with your record of mayhem——"

"Hold on there, Sphogeel," another member broke in. "I for one would like to hear this fellow's account of his experiences. It appears the activities of the Hagroon may have some significance——"

"I say let the Hagroon do as they like insofar as these fratricidal deviants are concerned!" Sphogeel came back. He seemed to be even more upset than his prejudices warranted. I could see the line he was taking now: he didn't intend even to give me a hearing. It was time for me to get my oar into the water.

"Whether you like it or not, Sphogeel," I cut across the hubbub, "the Imperium is a first-class, Net-traveling power.

55

Our two cultures were bound to meet sooner or later. I'd like to see our relations get off to a good start."

"Net-traveling?" the fat councillor queried. "You failed to mention that, Agent." He was looking sharply at Dzok.

"I was about to reach that portion of the briefing, Excellency," Dzok said smoothly. "Bayard had made the claim that although he was transported to the Hagroon line in a Hagroon shuttle, his people have a Web drive of their own. And, indeed, he seemed to be somewhat familiar with the controls of the primitive Hagroon machine."

"This places a different complexion on matters," the official said. "Gentlemen, I suggest we take no hasty action which might prejudice future relations with a Web power—"

"We'll have no dealings with the scum!" old Sphogeel shrilled, coming to his feet. "Our present policy of expl—"

"Sit down, Councillor!" the fat member roared, jumping up to face the thin one. "I'm well aware of the policies pertaining to this situation! I suggest we refrain from announcing them to the world!"

"Whatever your policy has been in the past," I interjected into the silence, "it should be reevaluated in the light of new data. The Imperium is a Net power, but there's no need of any conflict of interest—"

"The creature lies!" Sphogeel snarled, staring at me across the table. "We've carried out extensive reconnaissance in the entire Sapient quadrant—including the so-called Anglic Sector—and we've encountered no evidence whatever of native Web-transit capability!"

"The Zero-zero line of the Imperium lies within the region you call the Desolation," I said.

Sphogeel gasped. "You have the audacity to mention that hideous monument to your tribe's lust for destruction? That alone is sufficient grounds for your expulsion from the society of decent Hominoids!"

"How is that possible?" another asked. "Nothing lives within the Desolation. . . ."

"Another of the debased creature's lies," Sphogeel snapped. "I demand that the Council expel this degenerate at once and place a Class Two reprimand in the file of this agent—"

"Nevertheless," I yelled the councillors down, "a number of normal lines exist in the Blight. One of them is the seat of a Net government. As an official of that government, I ask that you listen to what I have to say, and give me the assistance I ask for."

"That seems a modest enough demand," the fat member said. "Sit down, Councillor. As for you, Bayard—go ahead with your story."

Sphogeel glowered, then snapped his fingers. A half-grown youth in unadorned whites stepped forward from an inconspicuous post by the door, listened to the oldster's hissed instructions, then darted away. Sphogeel folded his arms and glowered.

"I submit," he snapped. "Under protest."

Half an hour later I had finished my account. There were questions then—some from reasonable-sounding members like the chubby one whose name was Nikodo, others mere inflammatory remarks of the "Are you still beating your wife" type. I answered them all as clearly as I could.

"We're to understand then," a truculent-looking councillor said, "that you found yourself in a null-time level of your native continuum, having arrived there by means unknown. You then observed persons, presumably Hagroon, boarding transports, preparatory to departure. You killed one of these men, stole one of their crude Web-travelers, only to find yourself trapped. Arriving at the Hagroon world line, you were placed under confinement, from which you escaped by killing a second man. You now present yourself here with the demand that you be given valuable Authority property and released to continue your activities."

"That's not fairly stated, Excellency," Dzok started, but a dirty look cut him off.

"The man is a self-confessed double murderer," Sphogeel snapped. "I think—"

"Let him speak," Nikodo barked.

"The Hagroon are up to something. I'd say an attack on the Imperium from null time would be a likely guess. If you won't give us assistance, then I'm asking that you lend me transportation home in time to give a warning—"

The young messenger slipped back into the room, went to Sphogeel, handed him a strip of paper. He glanced at it, then looked up at me with a fierce glitter in his yellow eyes.

"As I thought! The creature lies!" he rasped. "His entire fantastic story is a fabric of deceit! The Imperium, eh? A Web Power, eh? Ha!" Sphogeel thrust the paper at the next councillor, a sad-looking, pale tan creature with bush muttonchop whiskers and no chin. He blinked at the paper, looked up at me with a startled expression, frowned, passed the paper along. When it reached Nikodo, he read it, shot me a puzzled look, reread it.

"I'm afraid I don't understand this, Bayard." His look bored into me now. His dark face was getting blackish-purple around the edges. "What did you hope to gain by attempting to delude this body?"

"Maybe if you'll tell me what you're talking about, I could shed some light on it," I said. Silently, the paper was tossed across to me. I looked at the crow tracks on it.

"Sorry. I can't read Xonijeelian."

"That should have been sufficient evidence in itself," Sphogeel growled. "Claims to be a Web operative, but has no language background . . ."

"Councillor Sphogeel had your statement checked out," Nikodo said coldly. "You stated that this Zero-zero world line lay at approximately our coordinates 875-259 within the area of the Desolation. Our scanners found three normal world lines within the desert—to that extent, your story contained a shred of truth. But as for coordinates 875-259 . . ."

"Yes?" I held my voice steady with an effort.

"No such world line exists. The uninterrupted sweep of the destroyed worlds blankets that entire region of the Web."

"You'd better take another look—"

"Look for yourself!" Sphogeel thrust a second paper across the table toward me—a glossy black photogram, far more detailed than the clumsy constructions used by the Imperial Net mapping service. I recognized the familiar oval shape of the Blight at once—and within it the glowing points that represented the worlds known as Blight-Insular Two and Three—and a third A-line within the Blight, unknown to me. But where the Zero-zero line of the Imperium should have been—was nothing.

"I think the Council has wasted sufficient time on this charlatan," someone said. "Take the fellow away."

Dzok was staring at me. "Why?" he said. "Why did you lie, Bayard?"

"The creature's purpose was clear enough," Sphogeel grated. "Ascribing his own base motivations to others, he assumed that to confess himself a citizen of a mere sub-technical race would mean he'd receive scant attention. He therefore attempted to overawe us with talk of a great Web power—a veiled threat of retaliation! Pitiful subterfuge! But nothing other than that would be expected from such a genetic inferior!"

58

"Your equipment's not working properly," I grated. "Take another scan—"

"Silence, criminal!" Sphogeel was on his feet again. He had no intention of losing the advantage his shock technique had gained him.

"Sphogeel has something he doesn't want known," I yelled. "He faked the shot—"

"That is not possible," Nikodo rapped out. "Wild accusations will gain you nothing, sapiens!"

"All I've asked for is a ride home." I flipped the scan photo across the table. "Take me there, and you'll see soon enough whether I'm lying!"

"Suicidal, he asks that we sacrifice a traveler and crew to play out his folly," someone boomed.

"You talk a lot about my kind's murderous instincts," I barked. "Where are the sapiens types here in this cosy little world of yours? In concentration camps, getting daily lectures on brotherly love?"

"There are no intelligent hairless forms native to Xonijeel," Nikodo snapped.

"Why not?" I rapped back at him. "Don't tell me they died out?"

"Their strain was a weak one," Nikodo said defensively. "Small, naked, ill-equipped to face the rigors of the glacial periods. None survived into the present era—"

"So you killed them off! In my world maybe it worked out the other way around—or maybe it was natural forces in both cases. Either way you slice it, it's ancient history. I suggest we make a new start now—and you can begin by checking out my story—"

"I say we put an end to this farce!" Sphogeel pounded on the table for attention. "I move the Council to a formal vote! At once!"

Nikodo waited until the talk died away. "Councillor Sphogeel has exercised his right of peremptory motion," he said heavily. "The vote will now be taken on the question, in the form to be proposed by the Councillor."

Sphogeel was still standing. "The question takes this form," he said formally. "To grant the demands of this sapiens . . ." he looked around the table as though gauging the tempers of his fellows.

"He's risking his position on the wording of the Demand Vote," Dzok hissed in my ear. "He'll lose if he goes too far."

". . . or, alternatively . . ." his eyes were on me now ". . . to order him transported to a sub-technical world line, to live out his natural span in isolation."

Dzok groaned. A sigh went around the table. Nikodo muttered. "If you'd only come to us honestly, sapiens," he started—

"The vote!" Sphogeel snapped. "Take the creature outside, Agent!"

Dzok took my arm, guided me out in the corridor. The heavy panels clicked behind us.

"I don't understand at all," he said. "Telling them all that rubbish about a Web power. You've prejudiced the Council hopelessly against you—and for what?"

"I'll give you a clue, Dzok," I said. "I don't think they needed any help—they already have their opinion of Homo sapiens."

"Nikodo was strongly inclined to be sympathetic," Dzok said. "He's a powerful member. But your senseless lies—"

"Listen to me, Dzok—" I grabbed his arm. "I wasn't lying! Try to get that through your thick skull! I don't care what your instruments showed. The Imperium exists!"

"The scanner doesn't lie, sapiens," Dzok said coldly. "It would be better for you to admit your mistake and plead for mercy." He pulled his arm free and smoothed the crease in the sleeve.

"Mercy?" I laughed, not very merrily. "From the kindly Councillor Sphogeel? You people make a big thing of your happy family philosophy—but when it gets right down to practical politics, you're as ruthless as the rest of the ape-stock!"

"There's been no talk of killing," Dzok said stiffly. "Relocation will allow you to live out your life in reasonable comfort—"

"It's not my life I'm talking about, Dzok! There are three billion people living in that world you say doesn't exist. A surprise attack by the Hagroon will be a slaughter!"

"Your story makes no sense, Anglic! Your claims have been exposed for the fancies they are! There is no such world line as this Imperium of yours!"

"Your instruments need overhauling. It was there forty-eight hours ago—"

The Council Chamber doors opened. The sentry listened to someone inside, then beckoned Dzok. The agent gave me a worried look, passed inside. The two armed men came to port arms, silently took up positions on either side of me.

"What did they say?" I asked. Nobody answered. Half a minute went by, like an amputee on crutches. Then the door opened again and Dzok came out. Two of the Council Members were behind him.

"An . . . ah . . . decision has been reached, Bayard," he said stiffly. "You'll be escorted to quarters where you'll spend the night. Tomorrow . . ."

Sphogeel shouldered past him. "Hesitant about performing your duty, Agent?" he rasped. "Tell the creature. His plots are in vain! The Council has voted relocation—"

It was what I had expected. I stepped back, slapped my gun into my hand—and Dzok's long arm swept down, caught me across the forearm with a blow like an axe, sent the slug gun bouncing off along the carpeted hall. I whirled, went for the short flit gun the nearest sentry was holding. I got a hand on it too—just as steel hooks clamped on me, hauled me back. A grayish-tan hand with black seal's fur on its back was in front of my face, crushing a tiny ampoule. An acrid odor hit my nostrils. I choked, tried not to breathe it in. . . . My legs went slack as wet rope, folded. I hit the floor without feeling it. I was on my back, and Dzok was leaning over me, saying something.

". . . regret . . . my fault, old boy . . ."

I made the supreme effort, moved my tongue, got out one word—". . . Truth . . ."

Someone pushed Dzok aside. Close-set yellow eyes stared into mine. There were voices:

". . . deep mnemonics . . ."

". . . finish the job . . ."

". . . word of honor as an officer . . ."

". . . devil take him. An Anglic's an Anglic . . ."

Then I was falling, light as an inflated balloon, seeing the scene around me swell, blur, fade into a whirling of lights and darkness that dwindled and was gone.

CHAPTER SIX

I watched the play of sunlight on the set of gauzy curtains at the open window for a long time before I began to think about who owned them. The recollection came hard, like a lesson learned but not used for a while. I had had a breakdown—a nervous collapse, that was it—while on a delicate mission to Louisiana—the details were vague—and now I

61

was resting at a nursing home in Harrow, run by kindly Mrs. Rogers....

I sat up, felt a dizziness that reminded me of the last time I had spent a week flat on my back after a difficult surveillance job in . . . in . . . I had a momentary half-recollection of a strange city, and many faces, and . . .

It was gone. I shook my head, lay back. I was here for a rest; a nice, long rest; then, with my pension—a sudden, clear picture of my passbook showing a balance of 10,000 gold Napoleons on deposit at the Banque Crédit de Londres flashed across my mind—I could settle somewhere and take up gardening, the way I'd always wanted to....

The picture seemed to lack something, but it was too much trouble to think about it now. I looked around the room. It was small, cheery with sunlight and bright-painted furniture, with hooked rugs on the floor and a bedspread decorated with a hunting scene that suggested long winter nights spent tatting by an open fire. The door was narrow, paneled, brown-painted wood, with a bright brass knob. The knob turned and a buxom woman with grey hair, cheeks like apples, a funny little hat made of lace, and a many-colored skirt that brushed the floor came in, gave a jump when she saw me, and beamed as though I'd just said she made apple pie like Mother's.

"Mr. Bayard! Ye're awake!" She had a squeaky voice as jolly as the whistle on a peanut stand, with an accent I couldn't quite place.

"And hungry, too, I'm guessing! Ye'd like a lovely bowl of soup, now wouldn't ye, sir? And maybe a dab of pudding after."

"A nice steak smothered in mushrooms sounds better," I said. "And, uh . . ." I had meant to ask her who she was, but then I remembered: kindly Mrs. Rogers, of course....

"A glass of wine, if it's available," I finished, and lay back, watching little bright spots dance before me.

"Of course, and a nice hot bath first. That'll be lovely, Mr. Bayard. I'll just call Hilda . . ." Things were a little hazy then for a few minutes. I was vaguely aware of bustlings and the twitter of feminine voices. Hands plucked at me, tugged gently at my arms. I made an effort, got my eyes open, saw the curve of a colored apron over a girlish hip. She was leaning across me, just getting my pajama jacket off. Beyond her, the older woman was directing two husky, blonde males in maneuvering something heavy below my line of sight. The girl straightened, and I caught a glimpse of a slim waist, a nicely rounded bosom and arm, a saucy face under straight-cut hair the color of clover honey. The two men finished and left, the motherly type with them. The girl fussed about for a minute, then followed the others, leaving the door open. I got up on one elbow, saw a six-foot-long enameled bathtub half full of water placed neatly on the oval rug, a big fluffy towel, a scrub brush, and a square cake of white soap on a small stool beside it. It looked inviting. I sat up, got my legs over the side of the bed, took deep breaths until the dizziness went away, then pulled off the purple silk pajama bottoms and stood, shakily.

"Oh, ye shouldn't try to walk yet, sir!" a warm contralto voice said from the doorway. Honey-hair was back, coming toward me with a concerned look on her pert features. I made a halfhearted grab for my pants, almost fell, sat down heavily on the bed. She was beside me now, with a strong hand under my arm.

"Gunvor and I've been worried about ye, sir. The doctor said ye'd been very sick, but when ye slept all day yesterday . . ."

I wasn't following what she said. It's one thing to wake up in an unfamiliar room and have a little trouble getting oriented; it's considerably different to realize that you're among total strangers, and that you have no recollection at all of how you got there. . . .

With her assistance, I made the three steps to the tub, hesitated before tackling the climb in.

"Just put your foot in, that's right," the girl was saying. I followed orders, stepped in and sat down, feeling too weak even to wince at the hot water. The girl perched on the stool beside me, tossed her head to get her hair back, reached for my arm.

"I'm Hilda," she said. "I live just along the road. It was exciting when Gunvor phoned and told me about yer coming, sir. It isn't often we see a Louisianan here—and a diplomat, too. Ye must lead the most exciting life! I suppose ye've been in Egypt and Austria and Spain—and even in the Seminole Nation." She chattered and sudsed me, as unconcernedly as a grandmother bathing a five-year-old. What little impulse to resist I may have had faded fast; I was as *weak* as a five-year-old, and it felt good to have this lively creature briskly massaging my back with the brush while the sun shone through the window and the breeze flapped the curtain.

". . . yer accident, sir?" I realized Hilda had asked a question—an awkward one. I had a powerful reluctance to admit that I had—or appeared to have—some sort of mild amnesia. I hadn't forgotten everything, of course. It was just that the details were hazy. . . .

"Hilda—the man that brought me here—did he tell you anything about me—about the accident? . . ."

"The letter!" Hilda jumped up, went across to a table decorated with red, yellow, blue, and orange painted flowers, brought back a stiff square envelope.

"The doctor left this for ye, sir. I almost forgot!"

I reached for it with a wet hand, got the flap open, pulled out a single sheet of paper on a fancy letterhead, formally typed:

"Mr. Bayard,
It is with deep regret and expressions of the highest personal regard that I confirm herewith your retirement for disability from the Diplomatic Service of His Imperial Majesty, Napoleon V . . ."

There was more—all about my faithful service and devotion to duty, regrets that I hadn't recovered in time for a personal send-off, and lots of hopes for a speedy convalescence. Included was the name of a lawyer in Paris who would answer all my questions, and if at any time he could be of assistance, etc. etc. The name at the end was unfamiliar—but then, of course, everybody knew Count Regis de Manin, Deputy Foreign Minister for Security. Good old Reggie. . . .

I read the letter twice, then folded it and crammed it back into the envelope. My hands were quivering.

"Who gave you this?" my voice came out hoarse.

"T'was the doctor, sir. They brought ye in the carriage, two nights since, and he was most particular about ye. A pity about yer friends having to hurry to catch the steam packet for Calais—"

"What did he look like?"

"The doctor?" Hilda resumed her scrubbing. "He was a tall gentleman, sir, handsomely dressed, and with a lovely voice. Dark he was, too. But I saw him only for a moment or two, and in the gloom of the stable-yard I couldn't make out more." She giggled. "But I did mark his eyes were close together as two hazelnuts in an eggcup."

"Was he alone?"

64

"There was the coachmen, sir—and I think another gentle-man riding inside, but—"

"Did Mrs. Rogers see them?"

"Only for a few moments, sir. They were in a shocking hurry...."

Hilda finished with the bath, dried me, helped me into clean pajamas, helped me stagger back to bed and tucked me in. I wanted to ask questions, but sleep came down over me like a flood from a broken dam.

The next time I woke up, I felt a little more normal. I got out of bed, tottered to the closet, found a suit of strange-looking clothes with narrow trousers and wide lapels, a shirt with ruffles at collar and wrist, shoes with tiny buckles.

But of course they weren't really strange, I corrected myself. Very stylish, in fact—and new, with the tailor's tag still in the breast pocket.

I closed the closet, went to the window for a look. It was still open, and late-afternoon sun glowed in the potted gera-niums on the sill. Below was a tidy garden, a brick walk, a white picket fence, and in the distance, a tall openwork church spire. There was an odor of fresh-cut hay in the air. As I watched, Hilda came around the corner with a basket in her hand and a shawl over her head. She had on a heavy, ankle-length skirt and wooden shoes painted in red and blue curli-cues. She saw me and smiled up at me.

"Hello there, sir! Have you had yer sleep out, now?" She came over, lifted the basket to show me a heap of deep red tomatoes.

"Aren't they lovely, sir? I'll slice ye some for dinner."

"They look good, Hilda," I said. "How long have I been asleep?"

"This last time, sir?"

"Altogether."

"Well, ye came about midnight. After we tucked ye in, ye slept all through the next day and night, and woke this morn-ing about ten. After yer bath ye went back, and slept till now—"

"What time is it?"

"About five—so that's another six hours and more." She laughed. "Ye've slept like one drugged, sir...."

I felt a weight slide off me like thawed snow off a steep roof. Drugged! I wasn't sick—I was doped to the eyebrows.

"I've got to talk to Gunvor," I said. "Where is she?"

"In the kitchen, plucking a fine goose for yer dinner, sir. Shall I tell her—"

"No, I'm getting dressed. I'll find her."

"Sir, are ye sure ye're feeling well enough—"

"I'm fine." I turned back to the closet, fighting the drowsiness that washed around me like thick fog. I got out the clothes, donned underwear, a loose-sleeved silk shirt and tight black pants of heavy cavalry twill, eased my feet into the slippers. Out in the narrow not-quite-straight passage papered in woodland scenes and decorated with framed tintypes, I followed the sounds of clattering crockery, pushed through a swinging door into a low-ceilinged, tile-floored room with a big black coal range, stainless steel sinks where a teen-age girl soaped dishes before a window with a flower box just outside, a glass-paneled door, a display of copper pots on the wall, and a big scrubbed-looking wooden table where Gunvor stood, working over the goose.

"Why, it's Mr. Bayard!" She blew a feather off her nose, looking flustered.

I leaned on the table for support, trying not to think about the buzzing in my head.

"Gunvor, did the doctor give you any medicine for me?"

"He did indeed, sir. The little drops for yer soup, and the white powders for yer other dishes—though since ye've taken no solid food as yet—"

"No more medicine, Gunvor." Everything was blacking out around me. I planted my feet, tried to will away the dizziness.

"Mr. Bayard, yer not strong enough yet—ye shouldn't be on yer feet!"

"Not . . . going back to bed. Need to . . . walk." I got out. "Get me outside . . ."

I felt Gunvor's arm under mine, heard her excited voice. I was vaguely aware of stumbling up steps, then the coolness of out-of-doors. I tried again, drew a couple of deep breaths, blinked away the fog.

"Better," I said. "Just walk me . . ."

Gunvor kept a running string of clucks and suggestions that I lie down right away. I ignored her, kept walking. It was a nice garden, with brick walks curving and meandering among the vegetable plots, past a rose bed along the side, under fruit trees at the far end, by a tempting bench under a thick-boled oak, and back to the kitchen door.

"Let's go around again." I tried not to lean on Gunvor this time. I was stronger; I could feel faint stirrings of appetite.

The sun was sinking fast, throwing long, cool evening shadows across the grass. After the third lap, I waited by the kitchen door while Gunvor fetched a pitcher from the brown wooden icebox and poured me a glass of cool cider.

"Now ye'll sit and wait for yer dinner, Mr. Bayard," Gunvor suggested anxiously.

"I'm all right now." I patted the hand she had laid on my arm.

She watched me anxiously as I started off. I breathed deep and tried to sort out my thoughts. Someone had brought me here, drugged, arranged to keep me that way—for how long I didn't know, but I could check that by examining Gunvor's medicine supply. Someone had also been tinkering with my memory. The question of who—and why—needed answering.

I made an effort to cut through the fog, place an authentic recollection. It was June here, I judged, from the tender leaves and the budding roses. Where had I been in May, or last winter? . . .

Icy streets, tall buildings grim in the winter night, but inside, warmth, cheer, color, the laughing faces of friendly people and the smile of a beautiful redhead, named . . . named . . .

I couldn't remember. The almost-recollection slipped away like a wisp of smoke in a sudden breeze. Someone had done a good job—using deep hypnotics, no doubt—of burying my recollections under a layer of false memories. Still, they hadn't done as well as they thought. It had taken me only a few hours to throw off the nebulous impressions of a dubious past. Perhaps—

I turned, hurried back to the house. Gunvor was hesitating over a plate of fresh-baked pastries. She ducked something under her apron as I stepped into the room.

"Oh! Ye startled me, sir . . ."

I went across and removed a saltshaker half-filled with a coarse white powder from her hand, tossed it into the wastebasket.

"No more medicine, I said, Gunvor," I patted her reassuringly. "I know the doctor gave you instructions, but I don't need it any more. But tell me, is there a . . ." I groped for a word. I didn't want to alarm her by asking for a brain doctor, and she wouldn't understand "psychiatrist." "A hypnotist?" I waited for signs of comprehension. "Someone who talks to troubled people, soothes them—"

"Ah, ye mean a mesmerist! But there's none here in the

village, alas. . . . Only Mother Goodwill," she added doubt-fully.

"Mother Goodwill?" I prompted.

"I've nothing against her, mind ye, sir—but there's those that talk of witchcraft. And I was reading just the other day in the Paris *Match* that ye can develop serious neuroses by letting unqualified practitioners meddle with yer psyche."

"You're so right, Gunvor," I agreed. "But it's only a little matter of a faulty memory—"

"Are ye troubled with that too, sir?" Her face lit up. "I'm that forgetful meself, sometimes I think I should have some-thing done—but then a regular mesmerist's so dear, and as for these quacks—"

"What about Mother Goodwill? Does she live near here?"

"At the other end of the village, sir. But I wouldn't recom-mend her—not for a cultured gentleman like yerself. Her cottage is very plain, and the old woman herself is something less than a credit to our village. Dowdy, she is, sir—no sense of style at all. And as for clothes—"

"I won't be overly critical, Gunvor. Will you take me to her?"

"I'll summon her here, sir, if ye're determined—but there's a licensed master mesmerist in Ealing, just an hour by coach—"

"Mother Goodwill will do, I think. How soon can you get her here?"

"I'll send Ingalill—but if it's all the same to ye, sir, let me have her up after dinner. I've just popped me goose in, and the pies are browning even now—"

"After dinner will be fine. I'll take a few more turns around the garden and develop an appetite worthy of your cooking."

After a second slab of blackberry pie buried in cream too thick to pour, a final mug of ground-at-the-table coffee, and a healthy snort of brandy with the flavor of a century in a dark cellar safely under my belt, I lit up a New Orleans cigar and watched as Hilda and Gunvor lit the oil lamps in the sitting room. There was a timid tap at the door, and Ingalill, the kitchen slavey, poked her face in.

"The old witch is here," she piped. "Gunvor, she's smoking a pipe. I think it's got ground-up salamander innards in it—"

"She'll hear ye, ye wretch," Hilda said. "Tell her to wait until her betters summon her—"

Ingalill yelped and jumped aside, and a bent-backed an-cient in a poke bonnet pushed in past her, one gnarled hand gripping a crooked stick on which she leaned. Bright black

68

eyes darted about the room, lit on me. I stared back, taking in the warty nose, toothless gums, out-thrust chin, and wisp of white hair hanging beside one hollow cheek. I didn't see a pipe, but as I watched she snorted a last wisp of smoke from her nostrils.

"Who has need of Mother Goodwill's healing touch?" she quavered. "But, of course, it'd be ye, sir, who's come such a strange, long way—and with a stranger, longer path still ahead. . . ."

"Phooie, I told you it was the new gentleman," Ingalill said. "What's in the basket?" She reached to lift a corner of the red and white checked cloth covering the container, yelped as the stick cracked across her knuckles.

"Mind yer manners, dearie," Mother Goodwill said sweetly. She shuffled to a chair, sank down, put the basket on the floor at her feet.

"Now, Mother Goodwill," Gunvor said, sounding agitated. "The gentleman only wants a little help with—"

"He'd draw aside the veil of the past, the future to read more clearly," the crone piped. "Ah, he did well to call on old Mother Gee. Now . . ." her tone became more brisk. "If ye'll pour me a dram, Gunvor, to restore me strength a mite—and then ye'll all have to clear out—except m'lord, the new gentleman, o' course." She grinned at me like a meat-eating bird.

"I'm not interested in the future," I started—

"Are ye not, sir?" the old woman nodded as though agreeing. "Then it's a strange mortal ye are—"

". . . But there are some things I need to remember," I bored on, ignoring the sales pitch. "Maybe under light hypnosis I can—"

"So . . . then it's the past ye'd glimpse, as I thought," she commented imperturbably. Gunvor was clicking glasses at the sideboard. She came over and handed the old woman a glass, then got busy clearing dishes from the table, with Ingalill and Hilda working silently beside her.

Mother Goodwill smacked her lips over the brandy, then waved an oversized brown-spotted hand.

"Away with ye, now, me chicks!" she quavered. "I feel the spirit coming over me! The power's flowing in the celestial field-coil! Strange visions are stirring, like phantom vipers in a pot! What's this? What's this? Ai, curious indeed, the things the spirits whisper to me now. . . ."

"Hmmmp! Ye can skip the spirits routine," Hilda said. "All Mr. Bayard wants from ye—"

"Get along with ye, girl," the old woman snapped, "or I'll

send a cramp that'll lock yer knees together that tight the fairest swain this side o' Baghdad'll not unlock 'em! All o' ye! Off, now!"

They went. Then the hag turned to me.

"Now, down to business, sir." She used a wheedling tone. "What were ye thinking o' giving the old woman for a handful of lost recollections? Is it a lover ye've forgot, the raptures of youth, the key to happiness once glimpsed and now forever gone a-glimmering?"

I was grinning at her. "You'll be well paid, but let's skip the rest of the routine. I'll get straight to the point. I have reason to believe I'm suffering from induced amnesia, probably the result of post-hypnotic suggestion. I'd like you to put me under and see if you can counter the block."

Mother Goodwill leaned forward, looked at me keenly.

"There's a strangeness about ye—something I can't put me finger on. It's as though yer eyes was focused on a horizon that other men can't see...."

"Granted I'm a strange character, but not so strange you can't hypnotize—or mesmerize me, I hope."

"Ye say ye've been tampered with, yer memories taken from ye. Who'd've done a thing like that to ye, lad—and why?"

"Maybe if you're successful, I'll find out."

She nodded briskly. "I've heard of such things. Spells of darkness, cast by the light of a bloodred moon—"

"Mother Goodwill," I cut in. "Let's get one thing straight: every time you mention spells, magic, dark powers, or geese, the fee goes down. I'm interested in straight scientific mesmerism. Okay?"

"What, good sir? Would ye tell the Mistress of Darkness how to ply her trade?"

The routine was beginning to get tiresome. "Maybe we'd better forget the whole thing." I reached in my pocket for a coin. "My mistake...."

"Are ye saying Mother Goodwill's a fraud, then?" Her voice had taken on a suspiciously mild note. I looked at her, caught a glint of light from an eye as black and bright as a polished opal. "D'ye think the old woman's out to trick ye, to play ye false, to gull ye fer a new fledged chick, to..." her voice droned on, coming from far away now, booming like surf in a sea cave echoing, echoing...

"... ten!"

My eyes snapped open. A woman with a pale, almost

70

beautiful face sat, leaning pensively on one elbow, a cigarette in her hand, watching me. Her dark hair was done up in a tight bun. Her plain white blouse was open at the collar, showing a strong, graceful neck. There was one dark curl against her forehead.

I looked around the room; it was dark outside now; a clock was ticking loudly somewhere.

"What happened to the old beldame?" I blurted.

The woman smiled faintly, waved a well-manicured hand toward a black cape on the chair beside her, a gnarled stick leaning against it.

"Rather warm for working in," she said in a low voice. "How are you feeling?"

I considered. "Fine. But—" I caught a glimpse of a wisp of stringy grey hair under the edge of the cloak. I got out of my chair, went over and lifted it. There was a warty rubber mask, a pair of gnarly gloves.

"What's the idea of the getup?"

"I find it helpful in my . . . business. Now—"

"You fooled me in a bad light," I said. "I take it Gunvor and the others are in on the gag?"

She shook her head. "No one ever sees me in a good light, Mr. Bayard—and no one wishes to approach too close, even then. They're simple people hereabouts. In their thoughts, warts and wisdom go together—so I fit their image of a village mesmerist, else none would seek my skill. You're the only one who shares my little secret."

"Why me?"

She looked at me searchingly. "You are a most unusual man, Mr. Bayard. A true man of mystery. You talked to me—of many things. Strange things. You spoke of other worlds, like this our own familiar plane, but different, alien. You talked of men like animals, clothed in shaggy hair—"

"Dzok!" I burst out. My hands went to my head as though to squeeze the recollections from my brain like toothpaste from a tube. "The Hagroon, and—"

"Calmly, calmly, Mr. Bayard," the woman soothed. "Your memories—if true memories they are, and not fever fancies—are there, intact, ready to be recalled. Rest, now. It was not easy for either of us, this stripping away of veils from your mind. A master mesmerist indeed was he who sought to bury your visions of strange paradises and unthinkable hells—but all lies exposed now." I looked down at her and she smiled.

"I am no journeyman practitioner myself," she murmured. "But all my skill was challenged this night." She rose, went to a framed mirror on the wall, gracefully tucked back a strand of hair. I watched her without seeing her. Thoughts of Barbro, the flaming figure in the dark storeroom, the escape with Dzok from the Hagroon cell were jostling each other, clamoring to be remembered, thought about, evaluated.

Mother Goodwill plucked her cape from the chair, swirled it about her shoulders, hunching into the posture of the hag she had been. Her white hands slipped the mask in place, fitting it to her nose and mouth. The gloves and wig followed, and now the bright eyes gazed at me from the wrinkled face of age.

"Rest, sir," the ancient face cackled. "Rest, sleep, dream, and let those restless thoughts seek out and know their familiar places once again. I'll attend ye on the morrow—there's more that Mother Goodwill would learn of the universes ye've told me lurk beyond the threshold of this drab world."

"Wait," I said. "I haven't paid you . . ."

She waved a veined hand. "Ye've paid me well in the stuff visions are wrought on, sir. Sleep, I say—and awake refreshed, strong, with your wits keened to razor's edge. For ye'll be needing all yer strength to face what waits ye in the days yet undawned."

She went out then. I went along the hall to my dark room, threw my clothes on a chair, fell into the feather-mattressed bed, and sank down into troubled dreams.

CHAPTER SEVEN

It was three days before I felt strong enough to pay my call on Mother Goodwill. Her cottage was a thatch-roofed rectangle of weathered stone almost lost under a tangle of wrist-sized rose vines heavy with deep red blossoms. I squeezed through a rusted gate, picked my way along a path overhung with untrimmed rhododendron, lifted the huge brass knocker, clanked it against the low black oak door. Through the one small, many-paned window, I caught a glimpse of the corner of a table, a pot of forgetmenots, a thick leather-bound book. There was a humming of bees in the air, a scent of flowers, and a whiff of fresh-brewed coffee. Not the traditional setting for calling on a witch, I thought. . . .

The door opened. Mother Goodwill, looking neat in a white shirt and peasant skirt, favored me with a sad smile, motioning me in.

"No Halloween costume today," I commented.

"You're feeling better, Mr. Bayard," she said drily. "Will you have a mug of coffee? Or is't not customary in your native land?"

I shot her a sharp look. "Skeptical already?"

Her shoulders lifted and dropped. "I believe what my senses tell me. Sometimes they seem to contradict each other." I took a chair at the table, glanced around the small room. It was scrupulously clean and tidy, furnished with the kind of rustic authenticity that would have had the ladies of the DAR back home oohing and aahing and overworking the word "quaint." Mother Goodwill brought the pot over, poured two cups, put cream and sugar on the table, then sat.

"Well, Mr. Bayard, is your mind clear this morning, your remembrance well restored?"

I nodded, tried the coffee. It was good.

"Don't you have some other name I could call you?" I asked. "Mother Goodwill goes with the fright wig and the warts."

"You may call me Olivia." She had slim, white hands, and on one finger a fine green stone twinkled. She sipped her coffee and looked at me, as though making up her mind to tell me something.

"You were going to ask me questions," I prompted her. "After I've answered them, maybe you'll clear up a few matters for me."

"Many were the wonders you babbled of in your delirium," she said. I heard a tiny clatter, glanced at her cup; a fine tremor was rattling it against the saucer. She put it down quickly, ducked her hands out of sight.

"Oft have I sensed that there was more to existence than this . . ." she waved a hand to take in everything. "In dreams I've glimpsed enchanted hills and my heart yearned out to them, and I'd wake with the pain of something beautiful and lost that haunted me long after. I think in your wild talk, there was that which made a certain hope spring up again—a hope long forgotten, with the other hopes of youth. Now tell me, stranger, that talk of other worlds, like each to other as new-struck silver pieces, yet each with a tiny difference—and of a strange coach, with the power to fly from one to the next—all this was fancy, eh? The raving of a mind sore vexed with meddling—"

"It's true—Olivia," I cut in. "I know it's hard to grasp at first. I seem to recall I was a bit difficult to convince once.

We're accustomed to thinking we know everything. There's a powerful tendency to disbelieve anything that doesn't fit the preconception."

"You spoke of trouble, Brion..." she spoke my name easily, familiarly. I suppose sharing someone's innermost thoughts tends to relax formalities. I didn't mind. Olivia without her disguise was a charming woman, in spite of her severe hairdo and prison pallor. With a little sunshine and just a touch of makeup—

I pulled myself back to the subject at hand.

She listened attentively as I told her the whole story, from Richthofen's strange interrogation to my sentencing by the Xonijeelians.

"So I'm stuck," I finished. "Without a shuttle, I'm trapped here for the rest of my days."

She shook her head. "These are strange things, Brion, things I should not believe, so wild and fantastic are they. And yet—I do believe...."

"From what little I've learned of this world line, it's backward technologically—"

"Why, we're a very modern people," Olivia said. "We have steam power—the ships on the Atlantic run make the crossing in nine days—and there are the balloons, the telegraph, and telephone, our modern coal-burning road cars which are beginning to replace the horse in many parts of the colonies, even—"

"Sure, I know, Olivia—no offense intended. Let's just say that in some areas we're ahead of you. The Imperium has the M-C drive. My own native world has nuclear power, jet aircraft, radar, and a primitive space program. Here you've gone in other directions. The point is, I'm stranded here. They've exiled me to a continuum I can never escape from."

"Is it so ill then, Brion? You have a whole world here before you—and now that the artificial barriers have been cleansed from your mind, you'll freely recall these wonders you left behind!" She was speaking eagerly now, excited at the prospect. "You spoke of aircraft. Build one! How marvelous to fly in the sky like a bird! Your coming here could mean the dawn of a new Age of Glory for the Empire!"

"Uh-huh," I said ungraciously. "That's great. But what about *my* world? By now the Hagroon have probably launched their attack—and maybe succeeded with it! My wife may be wearing chains now instead of pearls!" I got up,

74

stamped over to the window and stared out. "While I rot here, in this backwater world," I snarled.

"Brion," she said softly behind me. "You find yourself troubled—not so much by the threat to your beloved friends as by the quality of remoteness these matters have taken on. . . ."

I turned. "What do you mean, remote? Barbro, my friends, in the hands of these ape-men—"

"Those who tampered with your mind, Brion, sought to erase these things from your memory. True, my skill availed to lift the curse—but 'tis no wonder that they seem to you now as old memories, a tale told long ago. And I myself gave a command to you while yet you slept, that the pain of loss be eased—"

"The pain of loss be damned! If I hadn't been fool enough to trust Dzok—"

"Poor Brion. Know you not yet it was he who gulled you while you slept, planted the desire to go with him to Xonijeel? Yet he did his best for you—or so your memory tells."

"I could have taken the shuttle back," I said flatly. "At least I'd have been there, to help fight the bastards off."

"And yet, the wise ones, the monkey-men of Xonijeel, told you that this Zero-zero world did not exist—"

"They're crazy!" I took a turn up and down the room. "There's too much here I don't understand, Olivia! I'm like a man wandering in the dark, banging into things that he can't quite get his hands on. And now—" I raised my hands and let them fall, suddenly inexpressibly weary.

"You have your life still ahead, Brion. You will make a new place for yourself here. Accept that which cannot be changed."

I came back and sat down.

"Olivia, I haven't asked Gunvor and the others many questions. I didn't want to arouse curiosity by my ignorance. The indoctrination Dzok and his boys gave me didn't cover much—just enough to get me started. I suppose they figured I'd get to a library and brief myself. Tell me something about this world. Fill me in on your history, to start with."

She laughed—an unexpectedly merry sound.

"How charming, Brion—to be called upon to describe this humdrum old world as though it were a dreamer's fancy—a might-have-been, instead of dull reality."

I managed a sour smile. "Reality's always a little dull to whoever's involved in it."

"Where shall I begin? With Ancient Rome? The Middle Ages?"

"The first thing to do is establish a Common History date—the point at which your world diverged from mine. You mentioned 'The Empire.' What empire? When was it founded?"

"Why, the Empire of France, of course . . ." Olivia blinked, then shook her head. "But then, nothing is 'of course'," she said. "I speak of the Empire established by Bonaparte, in 1799."

"So far so good," I said. "We had a Bonaparte, too. But his empire didn't last long. He abdicated and was sent off to Elba in 1814—"

"Yes—but he escaped, returned to France, and led his armies to glorious victory!"

I was shaking my head. "He was free for a hundred days, until the British defeated him at Waterloo. He was sent to St. Helena and died a few years later."

Olivia stared at me. "How strange . . . how eerie, and how strange. The Emperor Napoleon ruled in splendor at Paris for twenty-three years after his great victory at Brussels, and died in 1837 at Nice. He was succeeded by his son, Louis—"

"The Duke of Reichstadt?"

"No; the Duke died in his youth, of consumption. Louis was a boy of sixteen, the son of the Emperor and the Princess of Denmark."

"And his Empire still exists," I mused.

"After the abdication of the English tyrant George, the British Isles were permitted to enter the Empire as a special ward of the Emperor. After the unification of Europe, enlightenment was brought to the Asians and Africans. Today, they are semiautonomous provinces, administered from Paris, but with their own local Houses of Deputies empowered to deal with internal matters. As for New France—or Louisiana—this talk of rebellion will soon die down. A royal commission has been sent to look into the complaints against the Viceroy."

"I think we've got the C. H. date pretty well pinned down," I said. "Eighteen-fourteen. And it looks as though there's been no significant scientific or technological progress since."

This prompted questions which I answered at length. Olivia was an intelligent and well-educated woman. She was enthralled by my picture of a world without the giant shadow of Bonaparte falling across it.

The morning had developed into the drowsy warmth of

noon by the time I finished. Olivia offered me lunch and I accepted. While she busied herself at the wood-burning stove, I sat by the window, sipping a stone mug of brown beer, looking out at this curious, anachronistic landscape of tilled fields, a black-topped road along which a horse pulled a rubber-tired carriage, the white and red dots of farmhouses across the valley. There was an air of peace and plenty that made my oddly distant recollection of the threat to the Imperium seem, as Olivia said, like a half-forgotten story, read long ago—like something in the book lying on the table. I picked up the fat, red leather-bound volume, glanced at the title:

THE SORCERESS OF OZ, by Lyman F. Baum.

"That's funny," I said.

Olivia glanced over at the book in my hands, smiled almost shyly.

"Strange reading matter for a witch, you think? But on these fancies my own dreams sometimes love to dwell, Brion. As I told you, this one narrow world seems not enough—"

"It's not that, Olivia. We've pretty well established that our C. H. date is early in the nineteenth century. Baum wasn't born until about 1855 or so—nearly half a century later. But here he is. . . ."

I flipped the book open, noted the publisher—Wiley & Cotton, New York, New Orleans, and Paris—and the date: 1896.

"You know this book, in your own strange world?" Olivia asked.

I shook my head. "In my world he never wrote this one. . . ." I was admiring the frontispiece by W. W. Denslow, showing a Glinda-like figure facing a group of gnomes. The next page had an elaborate initial "I" at the top, followed by the words: " '. . . summoned you here,' said Sorana the Sorceress, 'to tell you . . .' "

"It was my favorite book as a child," Olivia said. "But if you know it not, how then do you recognize the author's name?"

"He wrote others. THE WIZARD OF OZ was the first book I ever read all the way through."

"The Wizard of Oz? Not The Sorceress? How enchanting it would be to read it!"

"Is this the only one he wrote?"

"Sadly, yes. He died the following year—1897."

"Eighteen ninety-seven; that could mean . . ." I trailed off. The fog that had been hanging over my mind for days since I had awakened here was rapidly dissipating in the brisk wind of a sudden realization: Dzok and his friends had relocated me, complete with phony memories to replace the ones they'd tried to erase, in a world-line as close as possible to my own. They'd been clever, thorough, and humane. But not quite as clever as they thought, a bit less thorough in their research than they should have been—and altogether too humane.

I remembered the photogram the councillors had shown me—and the glowing point, unknown to Imperial Net cartographers, which represented a fourth, undiscovered world lying within the Blight. I had thought at the time that it was an error, along with the other, greater error that had omitted —the Zero-zero line of the Imperium.

But it had been no mistake. B-I Four existed—a world with a Common History date far more recent than the 15th century—the C. H. date of the closest lines beyond the Blight.

And I was there—or here—in a world where, in 1897 at least one man known in my own world had existed. And if one, why not another—or two others: Maxoni and Cocini, inventors of the M-C drive.

"Could mean what, Brion?" Olivia's voice jarred me back to the present.

"Nothing. Just a thought." I put the book down. "I suppose it's only natural that even fifty years after a major divergence, not everything would have been affected. Some of the same people would be born. . . ."

"Brion," Olivia looked at me across the room. "I won't ask you to trust me, but let me help you."

"Help me with what?" I tried to recapture the casual expression I'd been wearing up until a moment before, but I could feel it freezing on my face like a mud pack.

"You have made a plan; I sense it. Alone, you cannot succeed. There is too much that is strange to you here, too many pitfalls to betray you. Let me lend you what help I can."

"Why should you want to help me—if I were planning something?"

She looked at me for a minute without answering, her dark eyes wide in her pale, classic face.

"I've spent my life in search for a key to some other world . . . some dreamworld of my mind. Somehow, you seem to be a link, Brion. Even if I can never go there, it would

78

please me to know I'd helped someone to reach the unattainable shore."

"They're all worlds, just like this one, Olivia. Some better, some worse—some much, much worse. They're all made up of people and earth and buildings, the same old natural laws, the same old human nature. You can't find your dreamworld by packing up and moving on; you've got to build it where you are."

"And yet—I see the ignorance, the corruption, the social and moral decay, the lies, the cheats, the treachery of those who hold the trust of the innocent—"

"Sure—and until we've evolved a human society to match our human intelligence, those things will exist. But give us time, Olivia—we've only been experimenting with culture for a few thousand years. A few thousand more will make a lot of difference."

She laughed. "You speak as though an age were but a moment."

"Compared with the time it took us to evolve from an amoeba to an ape—or even from the first Homo sapiens to the first tilled field—it *is* a moment. But don't give up your dreams. They're the force that carries us on toward whatever our ultimate goal is."

"Then let me lend that dream concrete reality. Let me help you, Brion. The story they told me—that you had fallen ill from overwork as an official of the Colonial Office, that you were here for a rest cure—'tis as thin as a Parisian nightdress! And, Brion . . ." She lowered her voice. "You are watched."

"Watched? By whom—a little man with a beard and dark glasses?"

"'Tis no jest, Brion! I saw a man last night lurking by the gate at Gunvor's house—and half an hour since, a man well muffled up in scarves passed in the road yonder, as you supped coffee."

"That doesn't prove anything—"

She shook her head impatiently. "You plan to fly, I know that. I know also that your visit to me will arouse the curiosity of those who prison you here—"

"Prison me? Why, I'm as free as a bird—"

"You waste time, Brion," she cut me off. "What deed you committed, or why, I know not; but in a contest between you and drab officialdom, I'll support your cause. Now, quickly, Brion! Where will you go? How will you travel? What plan will—"

"Hold on, Olivia! You're jumping to conclusions!"

"And jump you must, if you'd evade the hounds of the hunter! I sense danger, closing about you as a snare about the roebuck's neck!"

"I've told you, Olivia—I was exiled here by the Xonijeelian Council. They didn't believe my story—or pretended not to. They dumped me here to be rid of me—they fancy themselves as humane, you know. If they'd meant to kill me, they had every opportunity to do so—"

"They sought to mesmerize your knowledge of the past away; now they watch, their results to judge. And when they see you restive, familiar of a witch—"

"You're no witch—"

"As such all know me here. 'Twas an ill gambit that brought you here by daylight, Brion—"

"If I'd crept out at midnight, they'd have seen me anyway—if they're watching me as you seem to think— and they'd have known damned well I wasn't satisfied with their hand-painted picture of my past."

"In any case, they'll like it not. They'll come again, take you away, and once again essay to numb your knowledge of the worlds, and of your past."

I thought that over. "They might, at that," I said. "I don't suppose it was part of their relocation program to have me spreading technical knowledge among the primitives."

"Where will you go, Brion?"

I hesitated; but what the hell, Olivia was right. I had to have help. And if she intended to betray me, she had plenty on me already.

"Rome," I said.

She nodded. "Very well. What is the state of your purse?"

"I have a bank account—"

"Leave that. Luckily, I have my store of gold Napoleons buried in the garden."

"I don't want your money—"

"Nonsense. We'll both need it. I'm going with you."

"You can't—"

"Can, and will!" she said, her dark eyes alight. "Make ready, Brion! We leave this very night!"

"This is crazy," I whispered to the dark, hooded figure standing beside me on the shadowed path. "There's no reason for you to get involved in this . . ."

"Hush," Olivia said softly. "Now he grows restless. See him

there? I think he'll cross the road now, more closely to spy us out."

I watched the dense shadows, made out the figure of a man. He moved off, crossed the road a hundred yards below the cottage, disappeared among the trees on our side. I shifted my weight carefully, itching under the wild getup Olivia had assembled for me—warty face, gnarly hands, stringy white hair, and all. I looked like Mother Goodwill's older brother—as ill-tempered an old duffer as ever gnashed his gums at the carryings-on of the younger generation. Olivia was done up like Belle Watling in three layers of paint, a fancy red wig, a purple dress that fit her trim figure like wet silk, and enough bangles, rings, beads and tinkly earrings to stock a gyfte shoppe.

"Hist—he steals closer now," my coconspirator whispered. "Another half minute..."

I waited, listening to the monotonous chirrup of crickets in a nearby field, the faraway *oo-mau* of a cow, the yapping of a farm dog. After dark, the world belonged to the animals.

Olivia's hand touched mine. "Now..." I followed as she stepped silently off. I had to crouch slightly to keep below the level of the ragged hedge. There was no moon, only a little faint starlight to help us pick a way along the rutted dirt road. We reached the end of the hedge, and I motioned Olivia back, stole a look toward the house. A head was clearly silhouetted against the faint light from the small side window.

"It's okay," I said in a low voice. "He's at the window—"

There was a crunch of gravel, and a light snapped on, played across the ruts, flashed over me, settled on Olivia.

"Here, woman," a deep voice growled. "What're ye doing abroad after bell-toll?"

Olivia planted a hand on her hip, tossed her head, not neglecting to smile archly.

"Aoow, Capting," she purred. "Ye fair give me a turn! It's only me old gaffer, what oi'm seein orf to the rile-trine."

"Gaffer, is it?" The light dwelt on me again briefly, went back to caress Olivia's sequinned bosom. "Haven't seen ye about the village before. Where ye from?"

"I float about, as ye might say, Major. A tourist, like, ye might call me—"

"On shank's mare, in the middle of the night? Queer idea o' fun, I call it—and with yer gaffer, too. Better let me see yer identity papers, ducks."

"Well, as it 'appens, I come away in such a rush, they seem to 'ave got left behind. . . ."

"Like that, is't?" I heard a snort from the unseen man behind the light—one of the roving security police who were a fixture of this world, I guessed. "Run off with a fistful o' spoons, did ye? Or maybe lifted one purse too many—"

"Nofink o' that sort! What cheek! I'm an honest, licensed tart, plying 'er profession and keeping her old gaffer, what oi'm the sole support of!"

"Never mind, love. I won't take ye in. A wee sample of yer wares, and I'll forget I ever saw ye." He came close, and a big hand reached out toward Olivia. She let out a sharp squeak and jumped back. The cop brushed past me. I caught a glimpse of a tricorn hat, a beak nose, loose jowls, a splash of color on the collar of the uniform. I picked my spot, chopped down hard across the base of his neck with the side of my hand. He yelped, dropped the light, stumbled to hands and knees. The stiff collar had protected him from the full force of the blow. He scrambled, trying to rise; I followed, kicked him square under the chin. He back-flipped and sprawled out, unconscious. I grabbed up the light and found the switch, flicked it off.

"Is he . . . badly hurt?" Olivia was staring at the smear of blood at the corner of the slack mouth.

"He'll have trouble asking for bribes for a few weeks." I pulled Olivia back toward the hedgerow. "Let's hope our snooper didn't hear anything."

We waited for a minute, then started off again, hurrying now. Far away, a spark of wavering, yellowish light moved across the slope of the hill beyond the village.

"That's the train," Olivia said. "We'll have to hurry!"

We walked briskly for fifteen minutes, passed the darkened shops at the edge of town, reached the station just as the puffing coal-burner pulled in. A severe-looking clerk in a dark uniform with crossed chest straps and coattails accepted Olivia's money, wrote out tickets by hand, pointed out our car. Inside we found wide seats upholstered in green plush. We were the only passengers. I leaned back in my seat with a sigh. The train whistle shrilled, a lurch ran through the car.

"We're on our way," Olivia breathed. She looked ecstatic, like a kid at the fair.

"We're just going to Rome," I said. "Not the land of Oz."

"Who can say whither the road of the future leads?"

CHAPTER EIGHT

At the Albergo Romulus, Olivia and I had adjoining rooms well up under the eaves, with ceilings that slanted down to a pair of dormer windows opening onto a marketplace with a handsome Renaissance fountain, the incessant flutter of pigeons' wings, and a day and night shrilling of excited Italian voices. We were sitting at the small table in my room, eating a late breakfast of pizzas, washed down with a musty red wine that cost so little that even the local begging corps could afford to keep a mild buzz on most of the time.

"The two men I'm interested in were born somewhere in northern Italy about 1850," I told Olivia. "They came to Rome as young men, studied engineering and electronics, and in 1893 made the basic discovery that gave the Imperium the Net drive. I'm gambling that if Baum managed to get himself born, and in the nineties was writing something pretty close to what he did in my world—and in the Zero-zero A-line too—then maybe Maxoni and Cocini existed here too. They didn't perfect the M-C drive, obviously—or if they did, the secret died with them—but maybe they came close. Maybe they left something I can use."

"Brion, did you not tell me that all the worlds that lie about your Zero-zero line are desolate, blasted into ruin by these very forces? Is it safe to tamper with such fell instruments as these?"

"I'm a fair shuttle technician, Olivia. I know most of the danger points. Maxoni and Cocini didn't realize what they were playing with. They stumbled on the field by blind luck—"

"And in a thousand million other worlds of might-have-been they failed, and brought ruin in their wake...."

"You knew all this when we left Harrow," I said shortly. "It's my only chance—and a damned poor chance it is, I'll admit. But I can't build a shuttle from scratch—there's a specially wound coil that's the heart of the field-generator. I've installed 'em, but I never tried to wind one. Maybe—if there was a Maxoni here, and a Cocini—and they made the same chance discovery—and they wrote up their notes like good little researchers—and the notes still exist—and I can find them—"

Olivia laughed—a charming, girlish laugh. "If the gods decree that all those *ifs* are in your favor—why then 'tis plain, they mean you to press on. I'll risk it, Brion. The vision of the Sapphire City still beckons me."

"It's the Emerald City, where I come from," I said. "But we won't quibble over details. Let's see if we can find those notes, first. We'll have plenty of time then to decide what to do with them."

An hour later, at the local equivalent of a municipal record center, a tired-looking youth in a narrow-cut black suit showed me a three-foot ledger in which names were written in spidery longhand—thousands of names, followed by dates, places of birth, addresses, and other pertinent details.

"*Sicuro, Signore,*" he said in a tone of weary superiority, "the municipality, having nothing to hide, throws open to you its records—among the most complete archives in existence in the Empire—but as for reading them . . ." he smirked, tweaked his hairline mustache. "That the Signore must do for himself."

"Just explain to me what I'm looking at," I suggested gently. "I'm looking for a record of Giulio Maxoni, or Carlo Cocini—"

"Yes, yes, so you said. And here before you is the registration book in which the names of all new arrivals in the city were recorded at the time identity papers were issued. They came to Rome in 1870, you said—or was it 1880? You seemed uncertain. As for me . . ." he spread his hands. "I am even more uncertain. I have never heard of these relatives—or friends—or ancestors—or whatever they might be. In them, you, it appears, have an interest. As for me—I have none. There is the book, covering the decade in question. Look all you wish. But do not demand miracles of me! I have duties to perform!" His voice developed an irritated snap on the last words. He strutted off to sulk somewhere back in the stacks. I grunted and started looking.

Twenty minutes passed quietly. We worked our way through 1870, started on 1871. The busy archivist peered out once to see what we were doing, withdrew after a sour look. Olivia and I stood at the wooden counter, poring over the crabbed longhand, each taking one page of about two hundred names. She was a fast reader; before I had finished my page, she had turned to the next. Half a minute later she gave a sharp gasp.

"Brion! Look! Giulio Maxoni, born 1847 at Paglio; trade, artificer—"

I looked. It was the right name. I tried not to let myself get

too excited—but my pulse picked up in spite of the voice of prudence whispering in my ear that there might be hundreds of Giulio Maxonis.

"Nice work, girl," I said in a cool, controlled voice that only broke twice on the three words. "What address?"

She read it off. I jotted it down in a notebook I had thoughtfully provided for the purpose, added the other data from the ledger. We searched for another hour, but found no record of Cocini. The clerk came back and hovered, as though we'd overstayed our welcome. I closed the book and shoved it across the counter to him.

"Don't sweat it, Jack," I said genially. "We're just making up a sucker list for mailings on budget funerals."

"Mailings?" He stared at me suspiciously. "Municipal records are not intended for such uses—and in any event—these people are all long since dead!"

"Exactly," I agreed. "A vast untapped market for our line of goods. Thanks heaps. I'll make a note to give you special treatment when your time comes."

We walked away in a silence you could have cut into slabs with a butter knife.

Maxoni had lived at number twelve, Via Carlotti, fourth floor, number nine. With the aid of a street map purchased from an elderly entrepreneur in a beret and a soiled goatee who offered us a discount on racy postcards, which I declined with regret, we found it—a narrow alley, choked with discarded paper cartons, vegetable rinds, overflowing garbage barrels, and shoeless urchins who dodged madly among the obstacles, cheerfully exchanging badinage which would have made Mussolini blush. Number twelve was a faded late Renaissance front of rusticated granite wedged between sagging, boarded-up warehouses no more than a hundred or so years old. Maxoni, it appeared, had started his career in the most modest quarters available. Even a century ago, this had been a slum. I pushed open the caked door, stepped into a narrow hall reeking of garlic, cheese, decay, and less pleasant things.

"It looks terrible, Brion," Olivia said. "Perhaps we'd best make enquiries first—"

A door opened and a round, olive face set in cushions of fat looked out, and launched into a stream of rapid Italian.

"Your pardon, Madam," I replied in the courtly accents I had learned from the Roman Ambassador to the Imperial court. "We are but foreigners, visiting the Eternal City for the

85

first time. We seek the apartment where once our departed relative dwelt, long ago, when the gods favored him with the privilege of breathing the sweet air of sunny Italy."

Her jaw dropped; she stared; then a grin the size of a ten-lira pizza spread across her face.

"*Buon giorno, Signore e Signorina!*" She squeezed out into the hall, pumped our hands, yelled instructions back into her flat—from which a mouth-watering aroma of ravioli emanated—and demanded to know how she could serve the illustrious guests of fair Italy. I gave her the number of the apartment where Maxoni had lived, ninety-odd years before, and she nodded, started up the narrow stair, puffing like the steam-engine that we had ridden across Europe for two days and nights. Olivia followed and I brought up the rear; admiring the deposits of broken glass, paper, rags and assorted rubbish that packed every step and landing, with a trail winding up through the center worn by the feet of centuries of tenants. I would have given odds that the bits Maxoni might have contributed were still there, somewhere.

At the top, we went along a narrow hall, past battered-looking doors with white china knobs, stopped at the one at the end.

"There is a tenant, Signore," the landlady said. "But he is away now, at his job in the fish market that I, Sophia Gina Anna Maria Scumatti, procured for him! Believe me, if I hadn't given him an ultimatum that the rent must be paid or out he'd go, he'd be sleeping now, snoring like a serviced sow, while I, Sophia Gina—"

"Undoubtedly the Signora has to endure much from ungrateful tenants," I soothed. I had a hundred lira note ready in my jacket pocket—the same oddly cut jacket that had been in the closet at Gunvor's house. I fished the bill out, tendered it with an inclination of the head.

"If the Signora will accept this modest contribution—"

Mama Scumatti puffed out her cheeks, threw out her imposing bosom.

"It is my pleasure to serve the guest of Italy," she started; I pulled the bill back.

"... but let it not be said that I, Sophia Gina Anna Maria Scumatti, was ungracious—" Fat fingers plucked the note from my hand, dropped it into a cleavage like the Grand Canyon. "Would the Signore and Signorina care to enter?" She fumbled a three-inch key from a pocket, jammed it into a keyhole you could have put a finger through, twisted it, threw the door wide.

"Vidi!"

I looked in at a collapsed cot snarled with dirty blankets, a broken-down table strewn with garishly colored comics, empty coffee cups, stained, finger-greased glasses, and a half-loaf of dry-looking bread. There was a bureau, a broken mirror with racing tickets tucked under the frame, a wooden Jesus dangling on the wall, and an assortment of empty wine and liquor bottles bearing the labels of inferior brands, scattered about the room. The odor of the place was a sour blend of unlaundered bedding, old socks, and a distillery infested with mice.

I looked at Olivia. She gave me a cool smile, turned to our hostess.

"May we go in?"

Sophia Gina wrinkled her brow at me. "My sister would like to go inside and . . . ah . . . commune with the spirit of our departed progenitor," I translated freely.

The black, unplucked eyebrows went up. "But, as the Signore sees, the room is occupied!"

"We won't touch a thing; just look at it. A very emotional moment for us, you understand."

A knowing look crept over the round face. She gave Olivia, still wearing her makeup and rings, an appraising once-over, then looked me in the eye; one eyelid dipped in an unmistakable wink.

"Ah, but naturally, Signore! You and your . . . sister . . . would of course wish to commune—in private. Another hundred lira, please." She was suddenly brisk. I forked over silently, trying to look just a little hangdog.

"I dislike to hurry the Signore," the concierge said as she shook the second note down into the damp repository. "But try to finish in say two hours, *si*? There is the chance that Gino will be back for lunch." An elbow the size and texture of a football dug into my side. Two fat, broken-nailed hands outlined an hourglass in the air; two small black eyes rolled; then Mama Scumatti was waddling off, a hippo in a black skirt.

"What said the fat scoundrel?" Olivia demanded.

"Just admiring your figure," I said hastily. "Let's take a look around and see what clues we can turn up."

Half an hour later Olivia stood in the center of the room,

87

still wrinkling her nose, hands on hips, a lock of hair curling down over her damp forehead.

" 'Twas a hopeless quest from the first," she said. "Let's be off, before my stomach rebels."

I dusted off my hands, grimy from groping on the backs of shelves and under furniture. "We've looked in all the obvious places," I said. "But what about the unlikely spots? We haven't checked for loose floorboards, secret panels, fake pictures on the wall—"

" 'Tis a waste of time, Brion! This man was not a conspirator, to squirrel away his secrets in the mattress! He was a poor young student, no more, living in a rented room—"

"I'm thinking of little things he might have dropped; a bit of paper that could have gotten stuck in the back of a drawer, maybe. Nobody ever cleans this place. There's no reason something like that couldn't still be here, even after all these years."

"Where? You've had the drawers out, rooted in the base of the chest, lifted that ragged scrap of rug, probed behind the baseboard—"

She trailed off; her eyes were on the boxed-in radiator set under the one small window. The wooden panels were curled, split, loose-fitting. We both moved at once. Olivia deftly set aside the empty Chianti bottles and the tin can half full of cigarette butts. I got a grip on the top board, lifted gingerly. The whole assembly creaked, moved out.

"Just a couple of rusty nails holding it," I said. "I'll lever it free. . . ."

A minute later, with the help of a wooden coat hanger lettered "Albergo Torino, Roma," I had eased the housing away from the wall, revealing a rusted iron radiator, a few inches of piping, enough dust devils to fill a shoe box—and a drift of cigarette butts, ticket stubs, bits of string, hairpins, a playing card, paper clips, and papers.

Olivia ooooed, went to her knees. I watched as she blew dust aside, fished out a folded menu, half a sheet of yellowed paper with numbers scribbled on it, an envelope with a postmark in the twenties addressed to one Mario Pinotti, two postcards with faded black-and-white photos of local tourist spots, and a brittle square of paper, blank on both sides.

"It was a good idea," I said. "Too bad it didn't pan out." Silently, I replaced the cover, put the bottles and ashtray back. "You were right, Olivia. Let's get back out in the street where we can get a nice wholesome odor of fresh garbage—"

"Brion, look!" Olivia was by the window, turning the blank scrap of paper at an angle to catch the sun. "The ink has faded, but there was something written here. . . ."

I came over, squinted at the paper. The faintest of faint marks were visible. Olivia put the paper on the table, rubbed it gently over the dusty surface, then held it up to the mirror. The ghostly outline of awkward penmanship showed as a grey line.

"Rub it a little more," I said tensely. "Careful—that paper's brittle as ash." She complied, held it to the mirror again. This time I could make out letters:

Instituzione Galileo Mercoledì Giugno 7. 3 P.M.

"Wednesday, June 7th," I translated. "This just might be something useful. I wonder what year that was?"

"I know a simple formula for calculating the day on which a given date must fall," Olivia said breathlessly. " 'Twill take but a moment . . ."

She nibbled at her lip, frowning in concentration. Suddenly her expression lightened. "Yes! It fits! June 7, 1871 fell on a Wednesday!" She frowned. "As did that date in 1899, 1911—"

"It's something—that's better than nothing at all. Let's check it out. The Galileo Institute. Let's hope it's still in business."

A dried-up little man in armbands and an eyeshade nibbled a drooping yellowed mustache and listened in silence, his veined hands resting on the counter top as though holding it in place as a barrier against smooth-talking foreign snoopers.

"Eighteen seventy-one. That was a considerable time in the past," he announced snappishly. "There have been many students at the Institute since then. Many illustrious scientists have passed through these portals, bringing glory to the name of Galileo." An odor of cheap wine drifted across from his direction. Apparently we had interrupted his midmorning snort.

"I'm not applying for admission," I reminded him. "You don't have to sell me. All I want is a look at the record of Giulio Maxoni. Of course, if your filing system is so fouled up you can't find it, you can just say so, and I'll report the fact in the article I'm writing—"

"You are a journalist?" He straightened his tie, gave the mustache a twirl, and eased something into a drawer out of sight behind the counter, with a clink of glass.

"Just give me the same treatment you'd accord any humble seeker after facts," I said loftily. "After all, the public is the owner of the Institute; surely it should receive the fullest attention of the staff whose bread and vino are provided by the public's largesse. . . ."

That got to him. He made gobbling sounds, hurried away, came back wheezing under a volume that was the twin to the municipal register, slammed it down on the counter, blew a cloud of dust in my face, and lifted the cover.

"Maxoni, you said, sir. 1871 . . . 1871 . . ." he paused, popped his eyes at me. "'That wouldn't be *the* Maxoni?" His natural suspicious look was coming back.

"Ahhh . . ." a variety of sudden emotions were jostling each other for space on my face. *"The* Maxoni?" I prompted.

"Giulio Maxoni, the celebrated inventor," he snapped. He turned and waved a hand at a framed daguerrotype, one of a long, sombre row lining the room. "Inventor of the Maxoni churn, the Maxoni telegraph key, the Maxoni Improved Galvanic Buggy Whip—it was that which made his fortune, of course—"

I smiled complacently, like an inspector who has failed to find an error in the voucher files. "Very good. I see you're on your toes here at the Institute. I'll just have a look at the record, and then . . ." I let it trail off as Smiley spun the book around, pointed out a line with a chewed fingernail.

"Here it is, right here. His original registration in the College of Electrics. He was just a lad from a poor farming community then. It was here at the Institute that he got his start. We were one of the first, of course, to offer lectures in electrics. The Institute was one of the sponsors of the Telegraphic Conference, later in that same year . . ." He rattled on with the sales pitch that had undoubtedly influenced many an old alumnus or would-be patron of the sciences to fork over that extra bundle, while I read the brief entry. The address in the Via Carlotti was given, the fact that Maxoni was twenty-four, a Catholic, and single. Not much help there. . . .

"Is there any record," I inquired, "as to where he lived—after he made his pile?"

The little man stiffened. "Made his pile, sir? I fear I do not understand. . . ."

"Made his great contribution to human culture, I mean," I amended. "Surely he didn't stay on at the Via Carlotti very long."

A sad smile twitched at one corner of the registrar's tight mouth.

"Surely the gentleman jests? The location of the Museum is, I think, well known—even to tourists."

"What museum?"

The gnome spread his hands in a gesture as Roman as grated cheese.

"What other than the museum housed in the former home and laboratory of Giulio Maxoni? The shrine wherein are housed the relics of his illustrious career."

Beside me, Olivia was watching the man's face, wondering what we were talking about. "Pay dirt," I said to her. Then:

"You don't have the address of this museum handy, by any chance?

This netted me a superior smile. A skinny finger pointed at the wall beside him.

"Number twenty-eight, Strada d'Allenzo. One square east. Any child could direct you."

"We're in business, girl," I said to Olivia.

"Ah ... what was the name of the paper you ... ah ... claim to represent?" the little man's voice was a nice mixture of servility and veiled insolence. He was dying to be insulting, but wasn't quite sure it was safe.

"We're with the Temperance League," I said, and sniffed loudly. "The Maxoni questions were just a dodge, of course. We're doing a piece entitled: 'Drinking on Duty, and What it Costs the Taxpayer.'"

He was still standing in the same position, goggling after us, when we stepped out into the bright sunshine.

The Maxoni house was a conservative, stone-fronted building that would have done credit to any street in the East Seventies back home. There was a neglected-looking brass plate set above the inner rail beside the glass-paneled door, announcing that the Home and Laboratories of the Renowned Inventor Giulio Maxoni were maintained by voluntary contributions to the Society for the Preservation of Monuments to the Glory of Italy, and were open 9—4, Monday through Saturday, and on Sundays, 1—6 P.M. A card taped to the glass invited me to ring the bell. I did. Time passed. A dim shape moved beyond the glass, bolts rattled, the door creaked open, and a frowzy, sleep-blurred female blinked out.

"It's closed. Go away," said a voice like the last whinny of

91

a dying plow horse. I got a foot into the narrowing space between the door and the jamb.

"The sign says—" I started brightly.

"Bugger the sign," the blurry face wheezed. "Come back tomorrow—"

I put a shoulder against the door, bucked it open, sending the charming receptionist reeling back. She caught her balance, hitched up a sagging bra strap, and raised a hand, fingers spread, palm facing her, opened her mouth to demonstrate what was probably an adequate command of Roman idiom—

"Ah—ah, don't say it," I cautioned her. "The Contessa here is unaccustomed to the vigor of modern speech. She's led a sheltered life, tucked away there in her immense palazzo at Lake Constance. . . ."

"Contessa?" A hideous leer that was probably intended as a simper contorted the sagging face. "Oh, my, if I only would've known her Grace was honoring our little shrine with a visit—" She fled.

"A portal guarded by a dragon," Olivia said. "And the fair knight puts her to rout with but a word."

"I used a magic spell on her. You're promoted to Contessa now. Just smile distantly and act aloof." I looked around the room. It was a standard entry hall, high-ceilinged, cream-colored, with a stained-glass window shedding colored light across a threadbare, once-fine rug, picking up highlights on a marble-topped table in need of dusting, twinkling in the cut-glass pendants of a rather nice Victorian chandelier. A wide, carpeted stairway led up to a sunlit landing with another stained-glass panel. A wide, arched opening to the left gave a view of a heavy table with pots of wax flowers and an open book with a pen and inkpot beside it. There were rows of shelves sagging under rows of dusty books, uncomfortable looking horsehair chairs and sofas, a fireplace with tools under a mantel on which china gimcracks were arranged in an uneven row.

"Looks like Maxoni went in for bourgeois luxury in a large way, once he got onto the buggy-whip boom," I commented. "I wonder where the lab is?"

Olivia and I wandered around the room, smelling the odor of age and dust and furniture polish. I glanced over a few of the titles on the shelves.

Experiments with Alternating Currents of High Potential and High Frequency by Nikola Tesla caught my eye, and a slim pamphlet by Marconi. Otherwise the collection seemed to consist of good, solid Victorian novels and bound volumes of sermons. No help here.

The dragon came back, looking grotesque in a housecoat of electric green—a tribute to Maxoni's field of research, no doubt. A layer of caked-looking makeup had been hastily slapped across her face, and a rose-bud mouth drawn on by a shaky hand. She laced her fingers together, did a curtsey like a trained elephant, gushed at Olivia, who inclined her head an eighth of an inch and showed a frosty smile. This example of aristocratic snobbishness delighted the old girl; she beamed so hard I thought the makeup was going to crack like plaster in an earthquake. A wave of an economical perfume rolled over me like a dust storm.

"Her Grace wishes to see the laboratories where Maxoni did his great work," I announced, fanning. "You may show us there at once."

She shouldered in ahead of me to get a spot nearer the duchess and with much waving of ringed hands and trailing of fringes, conducted us along a narrow hall beside the staircase, through a door into a weedy garden, along a walk to a padlocked shed, chattering away the whole time.

"Of course, the workrooms are not yet fully restored," she uttered, hauling a key from a baggy pocket. She got the lock open, stopped as she groped inside, grunted as she found the light switch. A yellowish glow sprang up. Olivia and I stared in at dust, lumpy shapes covered with tarpaulins, dust, heaped cartons, dust, grimed windows, and more dust.

"He worked *here*?"

"Of course it was not so cluttered then. We're short of funds, you see, your Grace," she got the sell in. "We haven't yet been able to go through the items here and catalogue them, dispose of the worthless things, and restore the laboratory to its original condition. . ." She chattered on, unabashed by Olivia's silence. I poked around, trying to look casual, but feeling far from calm. It was in this shed—or a near facsimile —that Maxoni had first made the breakthrough that had opened the worlds of alternate reality. Somewhere here, there might be . . . something. I didn't know what I was looking for: a journal, a working model not quite perfected . . .

I lifted the corner of the dust cover over a heaped table, glanced at the assortment of ancient odds and ends: awkward, heavy-looking transformers, primitive vacuum tubes, bits of wire—

93

A massive object at the center of the table caught my eye. I lifted the cover, reached for it, dragged it to me.

"Really, sir, I must insist that you disturb nothing!" my guardian hippo brayed in my ear. I jumped, let the tarp fall; dust whoofed into the air. "This is just as the professor left it, that last, fatal day."

"Sorry," I said, holding my face in what I hoped was a bland expression. "Looks like a collection of old iron, to me."

"Yes, Professor Maxoni was a bit eccentric. He saved all sorts of odd bits and pieces—and he was forever trying to fit them together. He'd had a dream, he used to tell my departed Papa—when he was alive, of course—the professor, I mean—and Papa too, of course—"

"Your father worked for Maxoni?"

"Didn't you know? Oh, yes, he was his assistant, for ever so many years. Many's the anecdote he could tell of the great man—"

"I don't suppose he's still living?"

"Papa? Dear Papa passed to his reward forty-three—or is it forty-four . . . ?"

"He didn't leave a journal, I suppose—filled with jolly reminiscenses of the professor?"

"No—Papa wasn't what you'd call a lit'ry man." She paused. "Of course, the professor himself was most diligent about his journal. Five big volumes. It's one of the great tragedies of the Society that we've not yet had sufficient funds to publish."

"Funds may yet be forthcoming, Madam," I said solemnly. "The Contessa is particularly interested in publishing just such journals as you describe."

"Oh!" The painted-on mouth made a lopsided O to match the exclamation. "Your Grace—"

"So if you'd just fetch it along, so that her Grace can glance over it . . ." I left the suggestion hanging.

"It's in the safe, sir—but I have the key—I know I have the key, somewhere. I had it only last year—or was it the year before . . . ?"

"Find it, my good woman," I urged. "Her Grace and I will wait patiently here, thrilling to the thought that it was in this very room that the professor developed his galvanic buggy-whip."

"Oh, no, that was before he took this house—"

"No matter; the journals, please."

"Wouldn't you rather come back inside? The dust here—"

"As I said, we're thrilling to it. Hurry back. . . ." I waved her through the door. Olivia looked at me questioningly.

"I've sent her off to find Maxoni's journals," I said. She must have noticed something in my voice.

"Brion, what is it?"

I stepped to the table, threw back the cover. The heavy assembly I had moved earlier dominated the scattering of articles around it.

"That," I said, letting the note of triumph come through, "is a Moebius-wound coil, the central component of the M-C drive. If I can't build a shuttle with that and the old boy's journals, I'll turn in my badge."

CHAPTER NINE

The workshop I rented was a twelve-by-twenty space under a loft opening off a narrow alleyway that wound from the Strada d' Allenzo to a side-branch of the Tiber, a trail that had probably been laid out by goats, back before Rome was big enough to call itself a town. The former occupant had been a mechanic of sorts. There were rusty pieces of steam-engine still lying in the corners, a few corroded hand tools resting among the dust-drifts on the sagging wall shelves at one side of the room, odds and ends of bolts and washers and metal shavings trodden into the oil-black, hard-as-concrete dirt floor. The old fellow who leased the premises to me had grumblingly cleared away the worst of the rubbish, and installed a large, battered metal-topped table. This, plus the Moebius coil, which I had bribed the Keeper of the Flame into letting me borrow, and the journals, constituted my lab equipment. Not much to start moving worlds with—but still, a start.

Olivia had gotten us rooms nearby, cheaper and better quarters than the Albergo Romulus. There was a small hot plate in her room, charcoal-fired; we agreed to husband our meager funds by having two meals a day in, and the other at one of the small neighborhood pasta palaces where the carafes of wine were put on the table as automatically as salt and pepper back home.

I started my research program by reading straight through all five journals, most of which were devoted to bitter comments on the current political situation—the capital had just been moved to Rome from Florence, and it was driving prices up—notes on some seemingly pointless researches into magnetism, the details of a rather complicated but strictly Platonic affair with a Signora C., and worried budgetary computations that enlisted my fullest sympathy.

Only in the last volume did I start to strike interesting passages—the first, tentative hints of the Big Secret. Maxoni had been experimenting with coils; winding them, passing various types and amounts of electric current through them, and attempting to detect results. If he'd known more modern physics, he'd never have bothered, but in his ignorance, he persevered. Like Edison trying everything from horsehair to bamboo splints as filaments for his incandescent bulb, Maxoni doggedly tried, tested, noted results, and tried again. It was the purest of pure research. He didn't know what he was looking for—and when he found it, he didn't know what it was—at least not in this world. Of course, there had been no Cocini here. I didn't know what the latter's role had been back in the Zero-zero world line. It would be an interesting piece of reading for me when I got back—if I got back—if there were any place to get back to—

I let that line of thought die. It wasn't getting me anywhere. The last volume of the journal yielded up its secrets, such as they were—a few scattered and fragmentary mentions of the coil-winding, and a line or two regarding strange manifestations obtained with the goldleaf electroscope when certain trickle currents were used.

A week had gone by, and I was ready to start the experimental phase. There were a few electrical supply houses in the city, mostly purveyors to the Universities and research institutes; electricity was far from the Reddy Kilowatt stage in this world. I laid in a variety of storage batteries, oscillators, coils, condensers, vacuum tubes as big and clumsy as milk bottles, plus whatever else looked potentially useful. Then, at Olivia's suggestion, I let her mesmerize me, take notes as I repeated everything my subconscious had retained of the training I'd had in Net Shuttle technology—which turned out to be twice as valuable as Maxoni's notes.

They were pleasant days. I rose early, joined Olivia for breakfast, walked the two blocks to the shop, and toiled until lunch, recording my results in a book not much different from the ones Maxoni had used a century earlier. This was not a world of rapid change.

Olivia would come by at noon or a little after, looking fresh and cool, and healthier now, with the Roman sun giving her face the color it had lacked back in Harrow. The basket on her arm would produce sandwiches, pizzas, fruit, a bottle of wine. I had a couple of chairs by this time, and we'd spread our lunch on the corner of my formidable workbench, with the enigmatic bulk of the coil lying before us like some jealous idol in need of placating.

Then an afternoon of cut and fit and note, with curious passersby pausing at the open door to look in and offer polite greetings and shy questionings. By the time a month had passed, I was deferred to by all the local denizens as a mad foreigner with more than a suggestion of the sorcerer about him. But they were friendly, often dropping off a casual gift of a bottle or a salami or a wedge of pungent cheese, with a flourish of Roman compliments. Each evening, by the time the sun had dropped behind the crooked skyline across the way, and the shop had faded into deep shadow hardly relieved by the single feeble lamp I had strung up, my eyes would be blurring, my head ringing, my legs aching from the hours of standing hunched over the table. I would solemnly close the door, attach the heavy padlock, ignoring the fact that the door was nothing but a few thin boards hung from a pair of rusted hinges held in place by bent nails. Then walk home past the shops and stalls, their owners busy closing up now, up the stairs to the flat for a quick bath in the rust-stained tub down the hall, then out with Olivia to the evening's treat. Sitting at the wobbly tables on the tile floors, often on a narrow terrace crowded beside a busy street, we talked, watched the people and the night sky, then went back to part at the flat door—she to her room, I to mine. It was a curious relationship, perhaps—though at the time, it seemed perfectly natural. We were coconspirators, engaged in a strange quest, half-detectives, half researchers, set apart from the noisy, workaday crowd all around us by the fantastic nature of the wildly impractical quest we were embarked on. She, for reasons of romantic fulfillment, and I, driven by a compulsion to tear through the intangible prison walls that had been dropped around me.

My estimate of Olivia's age had been steadily revised downward. At first, in the initial shock of seeing Mother Goodwill unmasked, I had mentally assigned her a virginal fortyishness. Later, bedizened in her harlot's finery—and enjoying every minute of the masquerade—she had seemed younger; perhaps thirty-five, I had decided. Now, with the paint scrubbed away, her hair cut and worn in a casual Roman style, her complexion warm and glowing from the sun and the walks, her figure as fine as ever in the neat, inexpensive clothes she had bought in the modest shops near our flat, I realized with a start one day, watching her scatter bread crumbs for the pigeons behind the shop and laughing at their clumsy waddle, that she was no more than in her middle twenties.

She looked up and caught me staring at her.

"You're a beautiful girl, Olivia," I said—in a wondering tone, I'm afraid. "What ever got you off on that Mombi kick?"

She looked startled, then smiled—a merrier expression than the Lady Sad-eyes look she used to favor.

"You've guessed it," she said, sounding mischievous. "The old witch in the *Sorceress of Oz*—"

"Yes, but *why?*"

"I told you: my business. Who'd patronize a Wise Woman without warts on her chin?"

"Sure—but why haven't you married?" I started to deliver the old saw about there being plenty of nice young men, but the look on her face saved me from that banality.

"Okay, none of my business," I said quickly. "I didn't mean to get personal, Olivia . . ." I trailed off, and we finished our walk in a silence which, if not grim, was certainly far from companionable.

Three weeks more, and I had assembled a formidable compilation of data—enough, I told Olivia when she came to the shop at ten P.M. to see what had kept me, to warrant starting construction of the secondary circuits—the portion of the shuttle mechanism with which I was most familiar.

"The big job," I said, "was to calibrate the coil—find out what kind of power supply it called for, what sort of field strength it developed. That part's done. Now all I have to do is set up the amplifying and focussing apparatus—"

"You make it sound so simple, Brion—and so safe."

"I'm trying to convince myself," I admitted. "It's a long way from simple. It's a matter of trying to equate a complicated assemblage of intangible forces; a little bit like balancing a teacup on a stream of water, except that I have a couple of dozen teacups, and a whole fire department's worth of waterworks—and if I threw full power to the thing without the proper controls . . ."

"Then what?"

"Then I'd set up an irreversible cataclysm—of any one of a

98

hundred possible varieties. A titanic explosion, that keeps on exploding: an uncontrolled eruption of matter from another continuum, like a volcano pouring out of the heart of a sun— or maybe an energy drain like Niagara, that would suck the heat away from this spot, freeze the city solid in a matter of minutes, put the whole planet under an ice cap in a month. Or—"

" 'Tis sufficient. I understand. These are fearsome forces you toy with, Brion."

"Don't worry—I won't pour the power into it until I know what I'm doing. There are ways of setting up auto-timed cutoffs for any test I run—and I'll be using trickle power for a long time yet. The disasters that made the Blight, happened because the Maxonis and Cocinis of those other A-lines weren't forewarned. They set her up and let her rip. The door to Hell has well-oiled hinges."

"How long—before you'll finish?"

"A few days. There isn't a hell of a lot to the shuttle. I'll build a simple box—out of pine slabs, if I have to—just something to keep me and the mechanism together. It'll be a big, clumsy setup, of course—not compact like the Imperial models—but it'll get me there, as long as the power flows. The drain isn't very great. A stack of these six volt cells will give me all the juice I need to get me home."

"And if the Xonijeel were right," she said softly, "if the world you seek lies not where you expect—what then?"

"Then I'll run out of steam and drop into the Blight, and that'll be the end of another nut," I said harshly. "And a good thing too—if I imagined the whole Imperium—"

"I know you didn't, Brion. But if, somehow, something has . . . gone wrong. . . ."

"I'll worry about that when I get to it," I cut her off. I'd been plowing along, wrapping myself up in my occupational therapy. I wasn't ready yet to think about the thousand gloomy possibilities I'd have to face when I stepped into my crude makeshift and threw the switch.

It was three evenings later, and Olivia and I were sitting at a window table in one of our regular haunts, having a small glass of wine and listening to the gentle night sounds of a city without neon or internal combustion. She'd been coming by the shop for me every evening lately; a habit that I found myself looking forward to.

"It won't be long now," I told her. "You saw the box. Just

bolted together out of wood, but good enough. The coil's installed. Tomorrow I'll lay out my control circuitry—"

"Brion . . ." her fingers were on my arm. "Look there!"

I twisted, caught a fleeting glimpse of a tall, dark figure in a long, full-skirted coat with the collar turned up, pushing past through the sparse pedestrian traffic.

"It was—him!" Olivia's voice was tight with strain.

"All right, maybe it was," I said soothingly. "Take it easy, girl. How sure are you—"

"I'm sure, Brion! The same terrible, dark face, the beard—"

"There are plenty of bearded men in Rome, Olivia—"

"We have to go—quickly!" She started to get up. I caught her hand, pulled her gently back.

"No use panicking. Did he see us?"

"I—think—I'm not sure," she finished. "I saw him, and turned my face away, but—"

"If he's seen us—if he *is* our boy—running won't help. If he didn't see us, he won't be back."

"But if we hurried, Brion—we need not even stop at the flat to get our things! We can catch the train, be miles from Rome by daylight—"

"If we've been trailed here, we can be trailed to the next town. Besides which, there's the little matter of my shuttle. It's nearly done. Another day's work and a few tests—"

"Of what avail's the shuttle if they take you, Brion?"

I patted her hand. "Why should anyone want to take me? I was dumped here to get rid of me—"

"Brion, think you I'm some village goose to be coddled with this talk? We must act—now!"

I chewed my lip and thought about it. Olivia wasn't being soothed by my bland talk—any more than I was. I didn't know what kind of follow-up the Xonijeelian Web Police did on their deportees, but it was a cinch they wouldn't look kindly on my little home workshop project. The idea of planting me here had been to take me out of circulation. They'd back their play; Olivia was right about that. . . .

"All right." I got to my feet, dropped a coin on the table. Out in the street, I patted her hand.

"Now, you run along home, Olivia. I'll do a little snooping, just to satisfy myself that everything's okay. Then—"

"No. I'll stay with you."

"That's silly," I said. "If there *is* any rough stuff, you think I want you mixed up in it? Not that there will be. . . ."

"You have some madcap scheme in mind, Brion. What is it? Will you go back to the workshop?"

"I just want to check to make sure nobody's tampered with the shuttle."

Her face looked pale in the light of the carbide lamp at the corner.

"You think by hasty work to finish it—to risk your life—"

"I won't take any risks, Olivia—but I'm damned if I'm going to be stopped when I'm this close."

"You'll need help. I'm not unclever in such matters."

I shook my head. "Stay clear of this, Olivia. I'm the one they're interested in, but you could get hurt—"

"How close are you to finishing your work?"

"A few hours. Then some tests—"

"Then we'd best be starting. I sense danger close by this night. 'Twill not be long ere they close their noose.

I hesitated for just a moment, then took her hand. "I don't know what I've done to earn such loyalty," I said. "Come on, we've got work to do."

We went to the flat first, turned on lights, made coffee. Then, with the rooms darkened, took the back stairs, eased out into a cobbled alley. Half an hour later, after a circuitous trip which avoided main streets and well-lit corners, we reached the shop, slipped inside. Everything looked just as I'd left it an hour earlier: the six-foot-square box, its sides half-slabbed up with boards, the coil mounted at the center of the plank floor, the bright wire of my half-completed control circuits gleaming in the gloom. I lit a lamp, and we started to work.

Olivia was more than clever with her hands. I showed her just once how to attach wire to an insulator; from then on she was better at it than I was. The batteries required a mounting box; I nailed a crude frame together, fitted the cells in place, wired up a switch, made connections. Every half hour or so, Olivia would slip outside, make a quick reconnaissance—not that it would have helped much to discover a spy sneaking up on us. I couldn't quite deduce the pattern of their tactics—if any. If we had been spotted, surely the shop was under surveillance. Maybe they were just letting me finish before they closed in. Perhaps they were curious as to whether it was possible to do what I was trying to do with the materials and technology at hand. . . .

It was well after midnight when we finished. I made a final

connection, ran a couple of circuit checks. If my research had been accurate, and my recollection of M-C theory correct, the thing *should* work. . . .

"It looks so . . . fragile, Brion." Olivia's eyes were dark in the dim light. My own eyeballs felt as though they'd been rolled in emery dust.

"It's fragile—but a moving shuttle is immune to any external influence. It's enclosed in a field that holds the air in, and everything else out. And it doesn't linger long enough in any one A-line for the external temperature or vacuum or what have you to affect it."

"Brion!" She took my arm fiercely. "Stay here! Risk not this frail device! 'Tis not too late to flee! Let the evil men search in vain! Somewhere we'll find a cottage, in some hamlet far from their scheming . . ."

My expression told her she wasn't reaching me. She stared into my eyes for a moment, then let her hand fall and stepped back.

"I was a fool to mingle dreams with drab reality," she said harshly. I saw her shoulders slump, the life go from her face. Almost, it was Mother Goodwill who stood before me.

"Olivia," I said harshly, "For God's sake—"

There was a sound from the door. I saw it tremble, and jumped for the light, flipped it off. In the silence, a foot grated on bricks. There was a sound of rusty hinges, and a lesser darkness widened as the door slid back. A tall, dark silhouette appeared in the opening.

"Bayard!" a voice said sharply in the darkness—an unmistakably Xonijeelian voice. I moved along the wall. The figure advanced. There was a crowbar somewhere near the door. I crouched, trying to will myself invisible, reached—and my fingers closed around the cold, rust-scaled metal. The intruder was two yards away now. I straightened, raised the heavy bar. He took another step, and I jumped, slammed the bar down solidly across the back of his head, saw a hat fly as he stumbled and fell on his face with a heavy crash.

"Brion!" Olivia shrieked.

"It's all right!" I tossed the bar aside, reached for her, put my arms around her.

"You have to understand, Olivia," I rasped. "There's more at stake here than anyone's dream. This is something I have to do. You have your life ahead. Live it—and forget me!"

"Let me go with you, Brion," she moaned.

"You know I can't. Too dangerous—and you'd halve my

102

chances of finding the Zero-zero line before the air gives out."
I thrust my wallet into her cloak pocket. "I have to go now."
I pushed her gently from me.

"Almost . . . I hope it fails," Olivia's voice came through the
dark. I went to the shuttle, lit the carbide running light,
reached in and flipped the warm-up switch. From the shadows, I heard a groan from the creature I had stunned.

"You'd better go now, Olivia," I called. "Get as far away
as you can. Go to Louisiana, start over—forget the Mother
Goodwill routine. . . ."

The hum was building now—the song of the tortured
molecules as the field built, twisting space, warping time,
creating its tiny bubble of impossible tension in the massive
fabric of reality.

"Goodby, Olivia. . . ." I climbed inside the fragile box,
peered at the makeshift panel. The field strength meter told me
that the time had come. I grasped the drive lever and threw it
in.

CHAPTER TEN

There was a wrenching sensation, a sputter of arcing current
through untried circuits. Then the walls flicked from view
around me, and I was looking out on the naked devastation
of the Blight. No need for view-screens here. The foot-wide
gaps between the rough slats gave me a panoramic view of a
plain of rubble glowing softly under the light of the moon; a
view that shifted and flowed as I watched, blackening into
burned ruins, slumping gradually into a lava-like expanse of
melted and hardened masonry and steel.

I unclenched my teeth, tried a breath. Everything seemed all
right. I was riding an egg crate across Hell, but the field was
holding, leashed by the mathematical matrices embodied in a
few hundred strands of wire strung just so from nail to nail
around my wooden cage. The massive Moebius coil bolted to
the floor vibrated nervously. I made an effort to relax; I had a
long ride ahead.

My half-dozen jury-rigged instruments were obediently giving readings. I looked at the trembling needles and tried to
think about what they represented. The only map I had was a
fuzzy recollection of the photogram the Xonijeelians had
showed me. If this *was* a fourth island in the Blight—and I
had already decided not to question that assumption—then I

was driving in what ought to be close to the correct "direction." Navigation in the Net depended on orientation with an arbitrary set of values—measurements of the strength of three of the seemingly infinite number of "fields" which were a normal part of the multiordinal continua. A reading of any three of these values should give a location. Noting the progressive changes in the interrelation of the values provided a plot across the Net—maybe. There was the little matter of calibrating my instruments, estimating my A-entropic velocity, testing my crude controls to see how much steering I could do, and determining how to bring the shuttle into identity square on target when and if I found a target—and all of this before the air became too foul to breathe. There was no problem of food, water, or a place to sleep: I'd be dead long before any such luxuries became necessary.

My first rough approximation from the data on the dials told me that I was moving along a vector at least 150 degrees off the calculated one. I made a cautious adjustment to one of my crude rheostats, winced as the sparks flew, watched the dials to see the results.

They weren't good. Either I was misinterpreting my readings, or my controls were even worse than I'd thought. I scribbled down figures, made some hasty interpolations, and came up with the discovery that I was blasting along at three times my calculated Net velocity, on a course that seemed to be varying progressively. My hastily rigged untested circuitry was badly out of balance—not far enough out to spill the leashed entropic force in a torrent of destruction, but too far out to be soothing.

I made another haphazard adjustment, checked readings. The needles wavered, one back-tracking down the scale, two others moving steadily upward. I made a herculean effort to recall all I'd ever known about emergency navigation, and concluded that I had described most of a full circle and was now headed back in the opposite direction. There wasn't much play left in my controls. I pushed the lever which served as rudder all the way to the left, watched as instruments responded—not enough.

Another ten minutes passed. My watch was ticking away, measuring off some unimaginable quality in my timeless, headlong plunge across the alternate realities. It was like the tooth-gritting wait while the lab technician probes around with his needle, looking for a vein. One second seemed to last forever.

Another reading. No doubt about it now, I was following a roughly spiral course—whether descending or ascending, I couldn't tell. The control circuits were sparking continuously; the stresses induced by the unnatural entropic loads were rapidly overheating the inadequate wiring. A junction box tacked to a two-by-four was glowing a dull red, and the wood under it was smoking, turning black. As I watched, pale flames licked, caught, ran up the wood. I pulled off my jacket, slapped at the fire uselessly. A wire melted through, dropped, spattered fire as it crossed other naked wires, then hung, welded into a new position.

For a heart-stopping instant, I braced myself for the lurching drop into identity with the towering pillars of fire thundering silently outside—then realized that, miraculously, the shuttle was still moving. I rubbed smoke-stung eyes, checked dials; the coarse had changed sharply. I tried to reconstruct the erratic path I had taken, work out a dead reckoning of my position. It was hopeless. I could be anywhere.

The scene beyond the shuttle walls was strange, not like anything I remembered from Blight exploration films I'd seen. A row of steep-sided black cones stretched away to the horizon, each glowing dull red about its crater rim, over which continuous wellings of lava spilled, while vast bubbles burst, sending up dense belches of brown smoke that formed a cloud obscuring the moon. Here, it appeared, a new fault-line had been created in the planet's crust, along which volcanoes sprouted like weeds in a new-ploughed field.

I had been on my way for about forty minutes now. With a pang of homesickness I pictured Olivia, back at the flat, alone. Suddenly I was remembering the days, the evenings we'd spent together, her unfailing spirit, her gentle touch, the line of her throat and cheek as we sat at a table, raising glasses in the long Roman twilight. . . .

I had had everything there a man needed for a good life. Maybe I'd been a fool to exchange it for this—a doomed ride on a hell-bound train to nowhere. Maybe. But there hadn't really been any choice. There were things in life a man had to do, or the savor was gone forever.

I was lost now, that was clear enough. For the last hour the shuttle had been charging across the continua blindly, describing an erratic course which varied every time a connection fused and created a new pattern in the control circuits. The post was still smouldering and smoking.

I had stretched out on the floor some time earlier, trying to find cleaner air. It was about gone now. I coughed with every breath, and my head kept up a steady humming, like a wornout transformer. I was picking up some interesting observations on the effects of modifying shuttle circuitry at full gallop—and observing some new country, never before explored by our Net Scouts—but the chances of my surviving to use it were dwindling with each passing minute. I had scratched a few lines of calculations on the floor with a fragment of charred wood. At the rate I was moving, I was deep in the Blight by now. Outside the ruined worlds flowed past, a panorama of doomsdays. The volcanoes were gone, shrunken to fiery pits that sparked and hurled fountains of fire into the black sky. I blinked, peering through shrouding mists of steam and smoke. Far away, a line of dark hills showed—new hills, created by the upheavals of this world's crust. The smoke thinned for a moment, gave me a clearer glimpse of the distant landscape—

Was that a hint of green? I rubbed at my eyes, stared some more. The hills, dim in the moonlight, seemed to show a covering of plant life. The nearby fire pits seemed quieter now, stilling to glowing pools of molten lava, glazing over into dullness. And there—! A scraggly bush, poking up at the rim of a crater—and another . . .

I drew a breath, coughed, got to hands and knees. The glow was fading from the scene. Unmistakable pinpoints of bright green were showing up everywhere. A shoot poked through the back soil, rose, twisted, unfurled a frond, shot up higher, extending leaf after leaf, in a speeded-up motion-picture sequence of growth, each frame a glimpse of a different A-line, varying by a trifle from the next, creating a continuous drama of change—a change toward life.

In its erratic wandering, it appeared, the shuttle had turned back toward the edge of the Blight. I watched, saw new shoots appear, spring up, evolve into great tree-ferns, giant cattails, towering palm-like trunks, along whose concrete-grey surfaces vines crept like small green snakes, to burgeon suddenly, embrace the vast tree in a smothering outburst of green, clamber over the crown, then sink down as the tree died and fell, only to turn on themselves, mound high, reach, capture a new host . . .

A jungle grew around me, nourished in the volcanic soil.

106

Orchids as big as dinner plates burst like popcorn, dropped, were replaced by others as big as washtubs. In the bright moonlight, I saw a flicker of motion—a new kind of motion. A moth appeared, a bright speck, grew until he was two feet across. Then the vast flower on which he perched closed over him in a frantic flurry of gorgeous wings and flamboyant petals.

Nearby, a wall of foliage bulged, burst outward. A head thrust through—gaping jaws like those of an immense rat closed on vines that coiled, choking. . . . The head changed, developed armor which grew out, blade-like, slicing through the ropes of living plant-fiber. Juice oozed, spilled; thorns budded, grew hungrily toward the animal, reached the furred throat—and recoiled, blunted, from armored hide. Then new leaves unfolded, reached to enfold the head, wrapping it in smothering folds of leathery green. It twisted, fought, tearing free only to be entoiled again, sinking down now, gone in a surging sea of green.

I coughed, choked, got to my feet, reached for the control panel—missed, and fell. The crack on the head helped for a moment. I tried to breathe, got only smoke. It was now or never. The worlds outside were far from inviting, but there was nothing for me in the shuttle but death by asphyxiation. I could drop into identity, make hasty repairs, study the data I had collected, decide where I was, and try again. . . .

Back to hands and knees; a grip on a board; on my feet now, reaching for the switch, find it in the choking smoke, pull—

There was a shock, a whirling, then a blow that sent me flying against shattering boards, into rubbery foliage and a gush of fresh air. . . .

I finished coughing, extricated myself from the bed of vines I found myself in, half expecting to see them reach for me; fortunately, however, the strange cause-and-effect sequences of E-entropy didn't apply here, in normal time.

In the gloom, I made out the shape of the flimsy box that had brought me here. It was canted against a giant tree trunk, smashed into a heap of scrap lumber. Smoke was boiling from under the heaped boards, and bright flames showed, starting along a wrist-thick vine, casting flickering lights and shadows on surrounding trees and underbrush. There was a board under my foot, still trailing a festoon of wires. I grabbed it up, struggled through to the fire, beat at the flames. It was a

107

mistake—the bruised stems oozed an inflammable sap which caught with bright poppings and cracklings. The main chassis of the broken shuttle was too heavy for me to try to drag back from the blaze. I tried to reach the coil, with some vague idea of salvage, but the fire was burning briskly now. The dry wood flamed up, sending fire high along the tree trunk, igniting more vines. Five minutes later, from a distance of a hundred yards, I watched a first-class forest fire getting underway.

The rain started then, too late to salvage anything from the shuttle, but soon enough to save the forest. I found shelter of sorts under a wide-leafed bush, listened for awhile to the drumming of the rain, then sank into exhausted sleep.

Morning dawned grey, wet, chilly, with water dripping from a billion leaves all around me. I crawled out, checked over assorted bruises, found everything more or less intact. I still had a slight rawness in the throat from the smoke, and somewhere I'd gotten a nice blister on the heel of my left hand, but that seemed a modest toll for the trip I had had.

The fire had burned out a ragged oval about a hundred feet across. I walked across the black stubble to the remains of the shuttle, surveyed the curled and charred boards, the blackened lump that had been the coil. The last, faint hope flickered and died. I was stranded for good, this time, with no handy museum to help me out.

There was a vague sensation in my belly that I recognized as hunger. I had a lot of thinking to do, some vain regrets to entertain, and a full quota of gloomy reflections on what was happening now back in the Imperial capital. But first, I had to have food—and, if my sketchy knowledge of jungles was any guide, a shelter of some sort against other inhabitants of the region that might consider me to be in that category.

And even before food, I needed a weapon. A bow and arrow would be nice, but it would take time to find a suitable wood, and I'd have to kill something for gut for the string. A spear or club was about all I'd be able to manage in my present state of technological poverty. And even for those, I'd need some sort of cutting edge—which brought me back to the stone age in two easy steps.

The ground had a slight slope to what I suspected was the east. I pushed my way through the thick growth—not as jungle-like as what I'd seen from the shuttle minutes before my crash landing, but not a nice picnicky sort of New

England wood either. I kept to the down-slope, stopping now and then to listen for gurgling streams or growling bears. The Boy Scout lore paid off. I broke through into a swampy crescent hugging a mud flat, with a meandering current at its center, fifty feet distant. Tight-packed greenery hung over the far side of the watercourse, which curved away around a spit of more grey mud. There were no stones in sight. Still, there was plenty of clay—good for pottery making, perhaps. I squatted, dipped up a sample. It was thin and sandy muck—useless.

There was ample room to walk beside the stream. I followed the course for several hundred yards, found a stretch of higher ground where the water came close to a bank of grassy soil. This would make as good a campsite as any. I pulled off my shoes, eased over the edge into the water, sluiced the worst of the soot and mud from myself and clothes. Turning back, I noticed a stratum of clean yellowish clay in the bank. It was the real stuff: smooth, pliable, almost greasy in texture. All I needed was a nice fire to harden it, and over which to cook my roasts, chops, fish fillets, et cetera—as soon as I had acquired the latter, using the weapons I would make as soon as I had an axe and a knife. . . .

It was almost sunset. The day's efforts had netted me one lump of flint, which I had succeeded in shattering into a hand axe and a couple of slicing edges that any decent flint worker would have tossed into the discard pile for archaeologists to quarrel over a few thousand years later. Still, they had sufficed to hack off two twelve-foot lengths of a tough, springy sapling, remove the twigs and leaves, and sharpen the small ends to approximate points. I had also gathered a few handfuls of small blackberry-like fruits which were now giving me severe stomach pains, and several pounds of the pottery clay which I had shaped into crude bowls and set aside for air drying.

The skies had cleared off in the afternoon, and I had built a simple shelter of branches and large leaves, and dragged in enough nearly-dry grass for a bed of sorts. And using a strip of cloth torn from my shirt, I had made a small fire-bow. With a supply of dry punk from the interior of a rotted tree, and a more or less smooth stone with a suitable hollow, I was now preparing to make a fire. My hardwood stick was less hard than I would have liked, and the bow was a clumsy makeshift, but it was better than just sitting and thinking. I crumbled the wood powder in the hollow, placed the pointed end of the stick against it with the bow string wrapped around it, and started in.

Ten minutes later, with the bow twice broken and replaced, the stick dulled, and the punk and my temper both exhausted, I gave it up for the night, crawled into my cosy shelter. Two minutes later, a bellow like a charging elephant brought me bolt upright, groping for a gun that wasn't there. I waited, heard a heavy body crashing through underbrush nearby, then the annoyed growl that went with the kind of appetite that preferred meat. There were a number of large trees in the vicinity. I found one in the dark with amazing speed and climbed it, losing a trifling few square feet of skin in the process. I wedged myself in a high crotch and listened to stealthy footsteps padding under my perch until dawn.

I found the tracks the next morning when I half-climbed, half-fell from the tree. They were deeply imprinted, too big to cover with my spread fingers, not counting the claws—on the prints, that is. Some kind of cat, I guessed. Down at the water's edge were more tracks: big hoof-marks the size of saucers. They grew 'em big in these parts. All I had to do was bag one, and I'd have meat for as long as I could stand the smell.

I was getting really hungry now. Following the stream, I covered several miles to the south, gradually working my way into more open country. There were plenty of signs of game, including the bare bones of something not quite as big as a London bus, with condor-like birds picking over them half-heartedly. I had my two spears and my stone fragments, and I was hoping to spot something of a size and ferocity appropriate to my resources—say a half-grown rabbit.

There was a sudden rattle of wings just in front of me, and a grousey-looking bird as big as a turkey took to the air. I advanced cautiously, found a nest with four eggs in it, speckled brown, three inches long. I squatted right there and ate one, and enjoyed every scrap. It would have been nice to have scrambled it but that was a minor consideration. The other three I distributed in various pockets, then went on, feeling a little better.

The country here was higher, with less underbrush and more normal-looking trees in place of the swampy jungle growth I'd started from. During high water, I imagined, the whole area where the shuttle lay would be submerged. Now I had a better view, off through the open forest, to what seemed like a prairie to the south. That's where the game would be.

Another half hour's walk brought me to the edge of a vast savannah that reminded me of pictures I'd seen of Africa, with immense herds grazing under scattered thorn trees. Here the trees were tall hardwoods, growing in clumps along the banks of the stream—and the animals were enough to make any zoo-keeper turn in his badge and start keeping white mice. I saw bison, eight feet at the shoulder; massive, tusked almost-elephants with bright pink trunks and pendulous lower lips; deer in infinite variety; and horses built like short-necked giraffes, ten feet high at the shoulder with sloping withers. There they were—and all I had to do was to stick them with my spear.

There was a low snort from somewhere behind me. I whirled, saw a head the size of a rhino's, set with two rows of huge, needlesharp teeth in a mouth that gaped to give me a view of a throat like the intake duct on a jet fighter. There was a body behind the head—ten feet or more of massively muscled tawny cat, with a hint of mane, faint stripes across the flanks, snow white throat, belly and feet. I took all these details in as the mighty carnivore looked me over, yawned, and paced majestically toward me, frowning across at the distant herds like a troubled politican wondering who to pay the bribe to.

He passed me up at a distance of thirty feet, moved out into the area, head high now, looking over the menu. None of the animals stirred. King Cat kept on, bypassed a small group of mastodons who rolled their eyes, switching their trunks nervously. He had his eye on the bison, among whom were a number of cuddly calves weighing no more than a ton. They moved restlessly now, forming up a defensive circle, like the musk-ox of the Arctic. The hunter changed his course, angling to the left. Maybe he was thinking better of it—

With the suddenness of thought, he was running, streaking across the grass in thirty-foot bounds, leaping now clear over the front rank of tossing horns to disappear as the herd exploded outward in all directions. Then he reappeared, standing over the body of a calf, one paw resting affectionately on the huddled tan corpse. The herd stampeded a short distance, resumed feeding. I let out a long breath. *That* was a hunter.

I jumped at a sound, spun, my hand with my trusty spear coming up automatically—

A brown rabbit the size of a goat stood poised on wiry legs, snuffling the air, showing long yellow rat-teeth. I brought the spear back, threw, saw it catch the creature in mid-leap as he whirled to flee, knocking him head over long white heels. I came pounding up, swung the second spear like a farmer's wife killing a snake, and laid him low.

Breathing hard, I gingerly picked up the bloody carcass, noting the gouge my spear had made. I looked around for a place to hole up and feast. Something black moved on my arm. A flea! I dropped the rabbit, captured the parasite, cracked him with a satisfying report. There were plenty more where that one came from, I saw, stirring around in the sparse hair on the foot-long ears. Suddenly I didn't want raw rabbit—or overgrown rat—for lunch.

As suddenly as that, the adrenalin I'd been getting by on for the past thirty-six hours drained away, left me a hungry, sick battered castaway, stranded in a hell-world of raw savagery, an unimaginable distance from a home which I knew I'd never see again. I had been bumbling along from one fiasco to the next, occupying my mind with the trivial, unwilling to face reality: the chilling fact that my life would end, here, in solitude and misery, in pain and fear—and that before many more hours had passed.

I lay under a tree, staring up at the sky, resting—I told myself—or waiting for another cat, less choosy, to happen along. I had had my chances—more than one—and I'd muffed them all. I'd gotten away clean in the Hagroon shuttle—then let it carry me helplessly along to their den-city, permitted myself to be captured without a struggle, thinking I'd learn something from the gorilla men. And after a combination of the enemy's stupidity and my luck had given me a new chance, a new shuttle—I'd guessed wrong again, let Dzok beguile me along to be sentenced to life in exile. And a third time—after my wild guesses had paid off—I had panicked, run from the enemy without waiting to test my home-built shuttle—and ended here. Each time I had made what seemed like the only possible choice—and each time I'd gotten farther from my starting point. Not farther in terms of Net distance, perhaps, but infinitely farther from any hope of rescue—to say nothing of my hope of warning the Imperial authorities of what was afoot.

I got to my feet, started back toward where I'd left the wreckage of the shuttle, with some half-formed idea of searching through the wreckage again—for what, I didn't know. It was the blind instinct of one who had absorbed all the disaster he can for a while, and who substitutes aimless action for the agony of thought.

It was harder now, plodding back over the ground I'd already covered. Following the course of the river, I passed the huge skeleton—abandoned now by the birds—reached the mud flat where the trampled remains of my crude hut gave a clear indication of the inadequacies of my choice of campsites. I had an idea of sorts then. Back at the shuttle there was a lump of metal—the remains of the original Maxoni coil. I might be able to use the material in some way—pound it out into spear-heads, or make a flint-and-steel for fire starting purposes. . . .

The impulse died. My stomach ached, and I was tired. I wanted to go home now, have a nice hot bath, crawl into bed, and be joined there by someone soft and perfumed and cuddly who'd smooth my fevered brow and tell me what a hell of a guy I was. . . .

It was easy to see the mechanics of schizophrenia at work here. From wishing, it was an easy jump to believing. I took a couple of deep breaths, straightened my back, and headed for the burn site. I'd try to retain my grip on reality a little longer. When it got unbearable, I knew the sanctuary of insanity would be waiting.

There were animal tracks across the blackened ground, hoof marks, paw prints, and—

I bent over, squinting to be sure. Footprints, human, or near enough. I knew how Robinson Crusoe had felt; the evidence of a fellow man gave me a sudden feeling of exposure along my backbone. I made it to the surrounding unburned wall of jungle in three jumps, slid down flat on the ground, and scanned the landscape. I tried to tell myself that this was a lucky break, the first real hope I'd had—but an instinct older than theories of the Brotherhood of Man told me that I had encountered the world's most deadly predator. The fact that we might be of the same species just meant competition for the same hunting ground.

My spear wasn't a handy weapon, and my skill with it wasn't anything to strike a medal in praise of. I checked my pocket for one of my stones, found a smashed egg. For a moment, the ludicrousness of the situation threatened to start me snickering. Then I heard a sound from nearby—in what

113

direction, I wasn't sure. I eased back, rose up far enough to scan the woods behind me. I saw nothing. I tried to think the situation through. If I was right—if it was a man who'd visited here—it was important to establish contact. Even a primitive would have some sort of culture—food, fire, garments of sorts, shelter. I had skills: pottery making, basket weaving, the principle of the bow. We could work out something, perhaps—but only if I survived the first meeting.

I heard the sound again, saw a deer-like creature making its way across the burn. I let out a breath I didn't know I'd been holding. There was no way of knowing how long ago the man prints had been made. Still, I couldn't lie here forever. I emerged, made a quick check of the burned-out shuttle. Everything was as I'd left it.

I took another look at the footprints. They seemed to be made not by a bare foot, but by a flat sandal of some sort. They came across the burn, circled the shuttle, went away again. On the latter portion of the trail, they clearly overlay my own booted prints. Whoever my visitor had been, he was following me—or had started out on my trail. It was a thought that did nothing for my peace of mind.

I tried to calm the instinct that told me to get as far from the spot as possible. I needed to meet this fellow—and on terms that I could control. I didn't want to kill him, of course—but neither did I want to try the palm outward "I friend" routine. That left—capture.

It was risky business, working out in the open. But then being alive was a risky business. If the man tracking me had followed my trail, then lost it somewhere on the high ground, it might be a matter of many hours before he came back here to cast about again—and I was sure, for some reason, that he'd do that. And when he did—

I had been working hard for two hours now, setting up my snare. It wasn't fancy, and if my proposed captive were any kind of woodsman—which he had to be, to survive here—it wouldn't fool him for a moment. Still, it was action of a sort—occupational therapy, maybe, but better than hiding under a bush and waiting—and it was helpful to my morale to imagine that I was taking the initiative.

The arrangement consisted of a shallow pit excavated in the soft soil, covered over with a light framework of twigs and leaves, and camouflaged with a scattering of blackened soil. I had done the digging with my bare hands, helped out by a board from the wreck, and the dirt had been heaped under the brush, out of sight behind the wall of foliage. The hole was no more than four feet deep, but that was sufficient for my purpose—to throw the intruder off-balance, and give me the drop on him sufficiently to open negotiations.

I was hungry enough now to scrape one of the smashed eggs from the lining of my pocket and eat it. But first I had to select my hiding place and get ready to act when the victim stepped into the trap. I picked a spot off to the left, arranged myself so as to be able to jump out at the psychological moment, and settled down to wait.

The pit was dug just in front of the wreckage, at the point where the opening to the interior would lead an inquisitive victim. I had dropped a lacy-edged hanky just inside the opening as an added attraction. It was one Olivia had lent me to mop my forehead during that last all-night session, and it still held a whiff of a perfume that would attract a primitive more surely than a scattering of gold coins. I had done all I could. The next step was up to the opposition.

I awoke from a light doze to see that it was late evening. The trees were black lacework against a red-gold sky, and the chirruping of crickets and the shrill *tseet! tseet!* of a bird were the only sounds against an absolute stillness—

And then the crackle of underbrush, the snap of broken twigs, the sound of heavy breathing. . . . I froze, trying to see through the gloom. He was coming. Hell, he was here! And making no effort at stealth. He was sure of himself, this native—which probably meant that here in his own stamping ground he was top carnivore. I tried to picture the kind of man who could stand up to the King Cat I'd seen, and gave it up as too discouraging. And this was the fellow I was going to trip up and then threaten with a broom handle. . . .

I swallowed the old corn husks that had gotten wedged in my throat, squinted some more. I made out a tall figure coming across the burned ground, stooping, apparently peering around—looking for me, no doubt. The thought gave me no comfort. I couldn't see what kind of weapon he had. I gripped my spear, tried to hold my breathing to a deep, slow rhythm. He was close now, pausing to glance over the shuttle, then turning toward the entrance hold. The handkerchief would be visible in the dim light, and the scent. . . . He took a step, another. He was close now, a vague, dark shape in deep shadow—

There was a choked yell, a crashing, a thud, and I was out

of my hidey-hole, stumbling across a tangle of roots, bringing my spear up, skidding to a halt before the pale torso and dark head of the man who struggled, scrabbling for a handhold, hip deep in my trap.

"Hold it right there!" I barked through clenched teeth, holding the spear ready with both hands, poised over the man who stood frozen now, a narrow-shouldered, long-armed figure, his face a dark blob under a white headpiece—

"I say, Bayard," Dzok's voice came. "You've led me a merry chase, I must say!"

CHAPTER ELEVEN

"It wasn't easy, old boy," Dzok said, offering me a second cup of a coffee-like drink he had brewed over the small fire he had built. "I can assure you I was in bad odor with the Council for my part in bringing you to Xonijeel. However, the best offense is a good defense, as the saying goes. I countered by preferring charges against Minister Sphogeel for compromise of an official TDP position, illegal challenge of an Agent's competence, failure to refer a matter of Authoritarian security to a full Board meeting—"

"I don't quite get the picture, Dzok," I interrupted. *"You* conned me into going to Xonijeel by promising me help against the Hagroon—"

"Really, Bayard, I promised no more than that I'd do my best. It was a piece of ill luck that old Sphogeel was on the Council that week. He's a notorious xenophobe. I never dreamed he'd go so far as to consign you to exile on the basis of a kangaroo hearing—"

"You were the one who grabbed my gun," I pointed out.

"Lucky thing, too. If you'd managed to kill someone, there'd have been nothing I could do to save you from being burned down on the spot. And I'm not sure I'd have wanted to. You *are* a bloodthirsty blighter, you know."

"So you followed me to B-I Four...."

"As quickly as I could. Managed to get myself assigned as escort to a recruitment group—all native chaps, of course—"

"Native chaps?"

"Ahhh ... Anglics, like yourself, captured as cubs ... er" ... babies, that is. Cute little fellows, Anglic cubs. Can't help warming to them. Easy to train, too, and damnably human—"

"Okay, you can skip the propaganda. Somehow it doesn't

116

help my morale to picture human slaves as lovable whities."

Dzok cleared his throat. "Of course, old chap. Sorry. I merely meant—well, hang it, man, what can I say? We treated you badly! I admit it! But—" he flashed me a sly smile. "I neglected to mention your rather sturdy hypnotic defenses against conditioning. I daresay you'd have had a bit more trouble throwing off your false memories if they'd known, and modified their indoctrination accordingly. And to make amends I came after you, only to find you'd flown the coop—"

"Why so mysterious? Why not come right up and knock on the door and say all was forgiven?"

Dzok chuckled. "Now, now, dear boy, can you imagine the reaction of a typical Anglic villager to *my* face appearing at the door, inquiring after a misplaced chum?"

I scratched at my jaw, itchy with two day's stubble. "All right, you had to be circumspect. But you could have phoned—"

"I could have remained hidden in the garret until after dark, then ventured out to reconnoiter, which is precisely what I did," Dzok said firmly. "I was ready to approach you at Mrs. Rogers' house, when you slipped away from me. I located you again at the cottage at the edge of the woods, but again you moved too quickly—"

"We spotted you creeping around," I told him. "I thought it was the Xonijeelian Gestapo getting ready to revise the sentence to something more permanent than exile."

"Again, I was about to speak to you on the road, when that fellow in the cocked hat interfered. Then you fooled me by taking a train. Had a devil of a time learning where you'd gone. I had to return to Xonijeel, travel to Rome, reshuttle to your so-called B-I Four line, then set about locating you. Fortunately, we maintain a permanent station in Italy, with a number of trusties—"

"More natives, I presume?"

"Quite. I say, old man, you're developing something of a persecution complex, I'm afraid—"

"That's easy, when you're persecuted."

"Nonsense. Why, you know I've always dealt with you as an equal ... "

"Sure, some of your best friends are people. But to hell with that. Go on."

"Umm. Yes. Of course, I had to operate under cover of darkness. Even then, it was far from easy. The Roman police are a suspicious lot. I turned you up at last, waited about

117

outside your flat, then realized what you were about, and hurried to your shop. You know what happened there. . . ." He rubbed his round skull gingerly. "Still tender, you know. Fortunately for me I was well wrapped up—"

"If you'd just said something . . ." I countered.

"Just as I opened my mouth, you hit me."

"All right, I'm sorry—sorrier than you know, considering what I went through after that. How the hell did you trail me here?"

He grinned, showing too many even white teeth. "Your apparatus, old boy. Fantastically inefficient. Left a trail across the Web I could have followed on a bicycle."

"You came to B-I Four ostensibly on a recruitment mission, you said?"

"Yes. I could hardly reveal what I had in mind—and it seemed a likely spot to find some eager volunteers for Anglic Sector duty—"

"I thought you had plenty of trusties you'd raised from cubs."

"We need a large quota of native recuited personnel for our Special Forces, chaps who know the languages and mores of the Anglic lines. We're able to offer these lads an exciting career, good pay, retirement. It's not a bad life, as members of an elite corps—"

"Won't it look a little strange when you come back without your recruits?"

"Ah, but I have my recruits, dear boy! Twenty picked men, waiting at the depot at Rome B-I Four."

I took a breath and asked The Question: "So you came to make amends? What kind of amends? Are you offering me a ride home?"

"Look here, Bayard," Dzok said earnestly. "I've looked into that business of Sphogeel's photogram—the one which clearly indicated that there is no normal A-line at the Web coordinates you mentioned—"

"So you think I'm nuts too?"

He shook his head. "It's not so simple as that. . . ."

"What's that supposed to mean?" My pulse was picking up, getting ready for bad news.

"I checked the records, Bayard. Three weeks ago—at the time you departed your home line in the Hagroon shuttle—your Zero-zero line was there, just as you said. Less than twelve hours later—nothing."

I gaped at him.

118

"It can mean only one thing. . . . I'm sorry to be the one to tell you this, but it appears there's been an unauthorized use of a device known as a discontinuity engine."

"Go on," I growled.

"Our own technicians devised the apparatus over a hundred years ago. It was used in a war with a rebellious province. . . ."

I just looked at him, waiting.

"I can hardly play the role of apologist for the actions of the previous generation, Bayard," Dzok said stiffly. "Suffice it to say that the machine was outlawed by unanimous vote of the High Board of the Authority, and never used again. By us, that is. But now it seems that the Hagroon have stolen the secret—"

"What does a discontinuity engine do?" I demanded. "How could it conceal the existence of an A-line from your instruments?"

"The device," Dzok said unhappily, "once set up in any A-line, releases the entropic energy of that line in random fashion. A ring of energy travels outward, creating what we've termed a probability storm in each A-line as the wave front passes. As for your Zero-zero line—it's gone, old man, snuffed out of existence. It no longer exists . . . "

I got to my feet, feeling light-headed, dizzy. Dzok's voice went on, but I wasn't listening. I was picturing the Hagroon stringing wire in the deserted garages of the Net Terminal; quietly, methodically preparing to destroy a world . . .

"Why?" I yelled. "Why? We had no quarrel with them. . . ."

"They discovered your Net capabilities. You were a threat to be eliminated—"

"Wait a minute! You said *your* bunch invented this discontinuity whatzit. How did the Hagroon get hold of it?"

"That, I don't know—but I intend to find out."

"Are you telling me they just put on false whiskers and walked in and lifted it when nobody was looking? That's a little hard to swallow whole, Dzok. I think it's a lot easier to believe you boys worked along with the Hagroon, hired them to do your dirty work—"

"If that were the case, why would I be here now?" Dzok demanded.

"I don't know. Why *are* you here?"

"I've come to help you, Bayard. To do what I can—"

"What would that be—another one-way ticket to some nice dead end where I can set up housekeeping and plant a garden

119

and forget all about what might have been, once, in a world that doesn't exist anymore because some people with too much hair decided we might be a nuisance and didn't want to take the chance—" I was advancing on Dzok, with ideas of seeing if his throat was as easy to squeeze as it looked. . . .

Dzok sat where he was, staring at me. "You don't have to behave like a complete idiot, Bayard, in spite of your race's unhappy reputation for blind ferocity—besides which, I happen to be stronger than you. . . ." He took something from the pocket of his trim white jacket, tossed it at my feet. It was my slug gun. I scooped it up.

"Still, if you actually are a homicidal maniac, go ahead. Don't bother to listen to what I have to say, or to wonder why I came here."

I looked at him across the fire, then thrust the gun into my pocket and sat down. "Go ahead," I said. "I'm listening."

"I gave the matter considerable thought, Bayard," Dzok said calmly. He poured himself another cup of coffee, sniffed at it, balanced it on his knee. "And an idea occurred to me. . . ."

I didn't say anything. It was very silent; even the night birds had stopped calling. Somewhere, far away, something bellowed. A breeze stirred the trees overhead. They sighed like an old man remembering the vanished loves of his youth.

"We've developed some interesting items in our Web Research Labs," Dzok said. "One of our most recent creations has been a special, lightweight suit, with its Web circuitry woven into the fabric itself. The generator is housed in a shoulder pack weighing only a few ounces. Its design is based on a new application of plasma mechanics, utilizing nuclear forces rather than the conventional magneto-electronic fields—"

"Sure," I snapped. "What does it have to do with me?"

"It gives the wearer Web mobility without a shuttle," Dzok continued. "The suit is the shuttle. Of course, it's necessary to attune the suit to the individual wearer's entropic quotient— but that in itself is an advantage: it creates an auto-homing feature. When the field is activated, the wearer is automatically transferred to the continuum of minimum stress—namely, his A-line of origin—or whatever other line his metabolism is attuned to."

"Swell. You've developed an improved shuttle. So what?"

"I have one here. For you." Dzok waved toward the bubble-shape of his standard Xonijeel model Web traveler—a far more sophisticated device than the clumsy machines of the

120

Imperium. "I smuggled it into my cargo locker—after stealing it from the lab. I'm a criminal on several counts on your behalf, old fellow."

"What do I do with this suit? Go snark hunting? You've already told me my world is gone—"

"There is another development which I'm sure you'll find of interest," Dzok went on imperturbably. "In our more abstruse researches into the nature of the Web, we've turned up some new findings that place rather a new complexion on our old theories of reality. Naturally, on first discovering the nature of the Web, one was forced to accept the fact that the narrow viewpoint of a single world-line did not represent the totality of all existence; that in a Universe of infinities, all possible things exist. But still, with the intellectual chauvinism inherent in our monolinear orientation, we assumed that the wavefront of simultaneous reality advanced everywhere at the same rate. That 'now' in one A-line was of necessity 'now' in every other—and that this was an immutable quality, as irreversible as entropy. . . ."

"Well, isn't it?"

"Yes—precisely as irreversible as entropy. But now it appears that entropy can be reversed—and very easily, at that." He smiled triumphantly.

"Are you saying," I asked carefully, "that you people have developed time travel?"

Dzok laughed. "Not at all—not in the direct sense you mean. There is an inherent impossibility in reversing one's motion along one's own personal time track. . . ." He looked thoughtful. "At least, I think there is—"

"Then what are you saying?"

"When one moves outward from one's own A-line, crossing other lines in their myriads, it is possible, by proper application of these newly harnessed subatomic hypermagnetic forces I mentioned to you, to set up a sort of—tacking, one might call it. Rather than traveling across the lines in a planiform temporal stasis, as is normal with more primitive drives, we found that it was possible to skew the vector—to retrogress temporally, to levels contemporaneous with the past of the line of origin—to distances proportional to the distance of normal Web displacement."

"I guess that means something," I said. "But what?"

"It means that with the suit I've brought you, you can return to your Zero-zero-line—at a time prior to its disappearance!"

It was nearly daylight now. Dzok and I had spent the last few hours over a chart laid out on the tiny navigation table in his shuttle, making calculations based on the complex formulation which he said represented the relationships existing between normal entropy, E-entropy, Net displacement, the entropic quotient of the body in question—me—and other factors too numerous to mention, even if I'd understood them.

"You're a difficult case, Bayard," the agent said, shaking his head. He opened a flat case containing an instrument like a stethoscope with a fitting resembling a phonographic pickup. He took readings against my skull, compared them with the figures he had already written out.

"I think I've corrected properly for your various wanderings in the last few weeks," he said. "Since it's been a number of years since your last visit to your original A-line—B-I three—I think we can safely assume that you've settled into a normal entropic relationship with your adopted Zero-zero line—"

"Better run over those manual controls with me again—just in case."

"Certainly—but let's hope you have no occasion to use them. It was mad of you, old chap, to set out in that makeshift shuttle of yours, planning to navigate by the seat of your pants. It just won't work, you know. You'd never have found your target—"

"Okay, but I won't worry about that until after I find out if I'm going to survive this new trip. What kind of margin of error will I have?"

Dzok looked concerned. "Not as much as I'd like. My observations indicated that your Zero-zero line was destroyed twenty-one days ago. The maximum displacement I can give you with the suit at this range is twenty-three days. You'll have approximately forty-eight hours after your arrival to circumvent the Hagroon. How you'll do that—"

"Is my problem."

"I've given it some thought," Dzok said. "You observed them at work in null time. From your description of what they were about, it seems apparent that they were erecting a transfer portal linking the null level with its corresponding aspect of normal entropy—in other words, with the normal continuum. They'd need this, of course, in order to set up the discontinuity engine in the line itself. Your task will be to give warning, and drive them back when they make their assault."

"We can handle that," I assured him grimly. "The trick will

be convincing people I'm not nuts...." I didn't add the disquieting thought that in view of the attitude of the Imperial authorities—at our last meeting—my own oldest friends included—it was doubtful whether I'd get the kind of hearing that could result in prompt action. But I could worry about that later too, after I'd made the trip—if I succeeded in finding my target at all.

"Now to fit the suit." Dzok lifted the lid of a wall locker, took out a limp outfit like a nylon diver's suit, held it up to me.

"A bit long in the leg, but I'll soon make that right...." He went to work like a skilled seamstress, using shears and a hot iron, snipping and re-sealing the soft woven plastic material. I tried it on, watched while he shortened the sleeves, and added a section down the middle of the back to accommodate my wider shoulders.

"Doesn't that hand-tailoring interfere with the circuits?" I asked, as he fussed over the helmet-to-shoulder fit.

"Not at all. The pattern of the weave's the thing—so long as I make sure the major connecting links are made up fast...."

He settled the fishbowl in place, then touched a stud on a plate set in the chest area of the suit, looked at the meters mounted on a small test panel on the table. He nodded, switched off.

"Now, Bayard," he said seriously. "Your controls are here ..."

It was full daylight now. Dzok and I stood on the grassy bank above the river. He looked worried.

"You're sure you understand the spatial maneuvering controls?"

"Sure—that part's easy. I just kick off and jet—"

"You'll have to use extreme care. Of course, you won't feel the normal gravitational effects, so you'll be able to flit about as lightly as a puff of smoke—but you'll still retain normal inertia. If you collide with a tree, or rock, it will be precisely as disastrous as in a normal entropic field."

"I'll be careful, Dzok. And you do the same." I held out my hand and he took it, grinning.

"Goodbye, Bayard. Best of luck and all that. Pity we couldn't have worked out something in the way of an alliance between our respective governments, but perhaps it was a bit

123

premature. At least now there'll be the chance of a future rapprochement."

"Sure—and thanks for everything."

He stepped back and waved. I looked around for a last glimpse of the morning sun, the greenery, Dzok's transparent shuttle, and Dzok himself, long-legged, his shiny boots mud-spattered, his whites mud-stained. He raised a hand and I pressed the lever that activated the suit. There was a moment of vertigo, a sense of pressure on all sides. Then Dzok flickered, disappeared. His shuttle winked out of sight. The strange, abnormal movement of normally immobile objects that was characteristic of Net travel started up. I watched as the trees wavered, edged about in the soil, putting out groping feelers toward me as though sensing my presence.

A hop, and I was in the air, drifting ten feet above the surface. I touched the jet-control and at once a blast of cold ions hurled me forward. I took a bearing, corrected course, and settled down for a long run.

I was on my way.

CHAPTER TWELVE

It was a weird trip across the probability worlds, exposed as I was to the full panoramic effects of holocausts of planetary proportions. For a while, I skimmed above a sea of boiling lava that stretched to the far horizon. Then I was drifting among fragments of the crust of a shattered world, and later I watched as pale flames licked the cinders of a burnt-out continent. All the while I sped northward, following the faint *be-beep!* of my autocompass, set on a course that would bring me to the site of Stockholm after four hours' flight. I saw great seas of oily, dead fluid surge across what had once been land, their foaming crests oddly flowing backwards, as I retrogressed through time while I hurled across A-space. I watched the obscene heaving and groping of monstrous life-forms created in the chaotic aftermath of the unleashed powers of the M-C field, great jungles of bloodred plants, deserts of blasted, shattered stone over which the sun flared like an arc-light in a black, airless sky. Now and again there would be a brief uprising of almost normal landscape, as I swept across a cluster of A-lines which had suffered less than the others. But always the outré element intruded: a vast, wallowing animal form, like a hundred-ton dog, or a mountainous, mutated cow, with extra limbs and lolling heads placed at random across the vast bulk through which bloodred vines grew, penetrating the flesh.

Hours passed. I checked my chronometer and the navigational instruments set in the wrist of the suit. I was close to my target and, according to the positional indicator, over southern Sweden—not that the plain of riven rock below me resembled the warm and verdant plains of Scania I had last seen on a hiking trip with Barbro, three months earlier.

I maneuvered close to the ground, crossed a finger of the sea that marked the location of Nyköping in normal space. I was getting close now. It was time to pick a landing spot. It wouldn't do to land too close to the city. Popping into identity on a crowded street would be unwise. I recognized the low, rolling country south of the capital now; I slowed my progress, hovered, waiting for the moment. . .

Abruptly, light and color blazed around me. I threw the main control switch, dropped the last few feet to a grassy hillside. It took me a moment to get the helmet clear; then I took a deep breath of cool, fresh air—the air of a world regained from twenty-two days in the past.

Down on the road, with the suit bundled under my arm, I flagged a horse-drawn wagon, let the driver ramble on with the assumption that I was one of those crazy sky-diver fellows. He spent the whole trip into town telling me how you'd never get him up in one of those things, then asked me for a free ride. I promised to remember him next time I was up, and hopped off at the small-town post office.

Inside, I gave a rambling excuse for my lack of funds to an ill-tempered looking man in a tight blue uniform, and asked him to put through a call to Intelligence HQ in Stockholm. While I waited, I noticed the wall calendar—and felt the sweat pop out on my forehead. I was a full day later than Dzok had calculated. The doom that hung over the Imperium was only hours away.

The plump man came back, with a thin man in tow. He told me to repeat my request to his superior. I began to get irritated.

"Gentlemen, I have important information for Baron Richthofen. Just put my call through—"

"That will not be possible," the slim fellow said. He had a nose sharp enough to poke a hole through quarter-inch plywood. It was red on the end, as though he'd been trying.

"You can charge the call to my home telephone," I said. "My name is Bayard, number 12, Nybrovägen—"

"You have identity papers?"

"I'm sorry; I've lost my wallet. But—"

"You place me in a difficult position," the thin fellow said, with a smile that suggested that he was enjoying it. "If the Herr is unable to identify himself—"

"This is important!" I rapped. "You have nothing to lose but a phone call. If I *am* on the level, you'll look like a damned fool for obstructing me!"

That got to him. He conferred with his chubby chum, then announced that he would check with the number I had given him in Stockholm, supposedly that of Herr Bayard. . . .

I waited while he dialed, talked, nodded, waited, talked some more in an undertone, placed the receiver back on the phone with a triumphant look. He spoke briefly to the other man, who hurried away.

"Well?" I demanded.

"You say that *you* are Herr Bayard?" he cooed, fingertips together.

"Colonel Bayard to you, Buster," I snapped. "This is a matter of life and death—"

"Whose life and death, ah. . . *Colonel* Bayard?"

"To hell with that . . ." I started around the counter. He leaned on one foot and I heard a distant bell sound. The fat man reappeared, looking flushed. There was another man behind him, a heavy fellow in a flat cap and gunbelt, with cop written all over him. He put a gun on me and ordered me to stand clear of the wall. Then he frisked me quickly—missing the slug gun which Dzok had restored—and motioned me to the door.

"Hold on," I said. "What's this farce all about? I've got to get that call through to Stockholm—"

"You claim that you are Colonel Bayard, of Imperial Intelligence?" the cop rapped out.

"Right the first time," I started.

"It may interest you to know," the thin postal official said, savoring the drama of the moment, "that Herr Colonel Bayard is at this moment dining at his home in the capital."

CHAPTER THIRTEEN

The cell they gave me wasn't bad by Hagroon standards, but that didn't keep me from pounding on the bars and yelling. I had my slug gun, of course—but since they wouldn't recognize it as a weapon even if I showed it, there was no chance of bluff. And I wasn't quite ready yet to kill. There were still several hours to go before the crisis and my call wouldn't take long—once they saw reason.

The fat man had gone away, promising that an official from the military sub-station at Södra would be along soon. Meantime I pounded and demanded that another call be put through—but nobody listened. Now my chance to use the gun was gone. The man with the keys kept to the outer office.

A slack-looking youth in baggy pants and wide blue and yellow suspenders brought me in a small smörgåsbord about noon. I tried to bribe him to make the call for me. He gave me a crooked smile and turned away.

It was well after dark when there was a sudden stir in the outer room of the jail. Then the metal door clanged open and a familiar face appeared—a field agent I had met once or twice in the course of my duties with Intelligence. He was a tall, worried-looking man, wearing drab civvies and carrying a briefcase. He stopped dead when he saw me, then came on hesitantly.

"Hello, Captain," I greeted him. "We'll all have a good chuckle over this later, as the saying goes, but right now I need out of here fast . . ."

The cop who had arrested me was behind him, and the fat man from the post office.

"You know my name?" the agent asked awkwardly.

"I'm afraid not—but I think you know me. We've met once or twice—"

"Listen to the fellow," the fat man said. "A violent case—"

"Silence!" the agent snapped. He came up close, looked me over carefully.

"You wished to place a call to Intelligence HQ," he said. "What did you wish to speak about?"

"I'll tell them myself," I snapped. "Get me out of here, Captain—in a hell of a hurry! This is top priority business!"

"You may tell me what it is you wished to report," he said.

"I'll report directly to Baron Richthofen!"

He lifted his shoulders. "You place me in an awkward position—"

"To hell with your position! Can't you understand plain Swedish? I'm telling you—"

"You will address an officer of Imperial Intelligence with more respect!" the cop broke in.

The agent turned to the two men behind him. "Clear out, both of you!" he snapped. They left, looking crestfallen. He turned back to me, wiped a hand across his forehead.

"This is very difficult for me," he said. "You bear a close resemblance to Colonel Bayard—"

"Resemblance! Hell, I *am* Bayard!"

He shook his head. "I was assured on that point, most specifically," he said. "I don't know what this is all about, my friend, but it will be better for you to tell me the whole story—"

"The story is that I have information of vital importance to the Imperium! Every minute counts, man! Forget the red tape! Get me a line to Headquarters!"

"You are an imposter. We know that much. You asked to have a call placed. A routine check at Colonel Bayard's home indicated that he was there—"

"I can't try to explain all the paradoxes involved. Just put my call through!"

"It is not possible to route every crank call to the Chief of Intelligence!" the man snapped. "What is this message of yours? If it seems to warrant attention, I will personally—"

"Let me talk to Bayard, then," I cut in.

"Ah, then you abandon your imposture?"

"Call it what you like. Let me talk to him!"

"That is not possible—"

"I didn't know we had anyone in the service as stupid as you are," I said clearly. "All right, I'll give you the message— and by all you hold sacred, you'd better believe me."

He didn't. He was polite, and heard me all the way through. Then he signaled for the jailer and got ready to leave.

"You can't walk out of here without at least checking my story!" I roared at him. "What kind of intelligence man are you? Take a look at the suit I had with me, damn you! That will show you I'm not imagining the whole thing!"

He looked at me, a troubled look. "How can I believe you? Your claim to be Bayard is a lie, and the story you tell is fantastic! Would *you* have believed it?"

I stared back at him.

"I don't know," I said, honestly. "But I'd at least have checked what I could."

He turned to the cop, who was back, hovering at the door. "You have this ... shuttle suit?"

The cop nodded. "Yes sir. I have it here on my desk. I've checked it for ..." his voice faded as he and the agent went out and the door shut behind them. For another half hour I paced the cell, wondering whether I should have shot a couple of them and tried to scare the cop into unlocking me; but from what I knew of the men of the Imperium, it wouldn't have worked. They were too damned brave for their own good.

Then the door clanged open again. A stranger was there this time—a small man with a runny nose and eyes, and glasses as thick as checkers.

". . . very odd, very odd," he was saying. "But meaningless, of course. The circuitry is quite inert ..."

"This is Herr Professor Doctor Runngvist," the agent said. "He's checked your ... ah ... suit, and assures me that it's crank work. A homemade hoax of some sort, incapable of any—"

"Damn you!" I yelled. "Sure the suit's inert—without me in it! I'm part of the circuitry! It's attuned to me!"

"Eh? Tuned to you? A part of the circuitry?" The old man adjusted his glasses at an angle to get a better view of me.

"Look, pops, this is a highly sophisticated device. It utilizes the wearer's somatic and neural fields as a part of the total circuitry. Without me inside, it won't work. Let me have it. I'll demonstrate it for you—"

"Sorry, I can't allow that," the agent said quickly. "Look here, fellow, hadn't you better drop this show now, and tell me what it's all about?" You're in pretty deep water already, I'd say, impersonating an officer—"

"You know Bayard, on sight, don't you?" I cut in.

"Yes ..."

"Do I look like him?"

He looked worried. "Yes, to an extent. I presume it was that which inspired this imposture, but—"

"Listen to me, Captain," I said as levelly as I could through the bars. "This is the biggest crisis the Imperium has faced since Chief Inspector Bale ran amok...."

The captain frowned. "How did you know of that?"

"I was there. My name's Bayard, remember? Now get me out of here—"

There was a shrilling of a telephone bell in the outer room. Feet clumped. Voices rumbled. Then the door flew open.

"Inspector! It's a call—from Stockholm. . . ."

My inquisitors turned. "Yes?"

"That fellow—Colonel Bayard!" an excited voice said. Someone shushed him. They stood in the hall, conversing in whispers. Then the intelligence captain came back with the cop behind him.

"You'd better start telling all you know," he snapped, looking grimmer than ever.

"What's happened?"

"Stockholm is under attack by an armed force of undetermined size!"

It was close to midnight now. I had been looking for a chance for a break for the past hour, but Captain Burman, the agent, was taking no chances. He had locked the outer door to the cell block and nobody was allowed even to come close to my cell. I think he was beginning to suspect that everything wasn't as simple as it appeared.

I watched the door across the aisle as a key clattered in it and it swung wide. It was Burman, white-faced, and two strangers, both in civilian clothes. My wrist tensed, ready to flip the gun into my palm, but they kept their distance.

"This is the man." Burman waved at me like a tenant complaining about a prowler. "I've gotten nothing from him but nonsense—or what I thought was nonsense, until now!"

The newcomers looked me over. One was a short, thick-set, hairless man in wide lapels and baggy-kneed pants. The other was trim, neat, well set up. I decided to make my pitch to the former. No underling could afford to look that messy.

"Listen, you," I started. "I'm Colonel Bayard, of Imperial Intelligence—

"I will listen, of that you may be assured," the little man said. "Start at the beginning and repeat what you have told the Captain."

"It's too late for talk." I flipped the gun into my hand. All three of them jumped, and a heavy automatic appeared in the snappy dresser's hand.

"Ever seen one of these before?" I showed the slug gun, keeping the armed man covered.

The thick man jerked his head in a quick nod.

"Then you know they're only issued to a few people in Net Surveillance work—including me. I could have shot my way out of here when I first arrived, but I thought I'd get a fair hearing without killing anybody. Now its too late for humanitarianism. One of you open up, or I start shooting—and I'm faster than you are, Buster," I added for the benefit of the tall man with the gun.

"Here, you're only making it worse—"

"It couldn't be worse. Get the key. Call that dumb flatfoot out front."

The thick man shook his head. "Shoot then, sir. Major Gunnarson will then be forced to return your fire, and so two men will die. But I will not release you."

"Why not? You can watch me. All I want to do is call Intelligence—"

"I do not know what set of signals you may have worked out, or with whom, and I do not intend to find out at the expense of the Imperial security."

"There's not any Imperial security, as long as you keep me here. I've told my story to Burman! Take action! Do something!"

"I have already attempted to relay your statement to Baron Richthofen at Stockholm," the rumpled man said.

"What do you mean, attempted?"

"Just that. I was unable to get through. All telephonic connection is broken, I found. I sent a messenger. He failed to return. Another messenger has reached me but now. He was dispatched an hour ago, and heard the news over his auto radio set just before . . ."

"Just before what?"

"Before the gas attack," he said in a harsh voice. Abruptly there was a gun in his hand—a heavy revolver. He had drawn it so quickly that I couldn't even say where he'd gotten it.

"Now, tell me all you know of these matters, Mr. Bayard, or whatever your name might be! You have ten seconds to begin!"

I kept my gun on his partner. I knew that if I moved it as much as a millimeter, the baggy man would gun me down. I tried to match the steely look in his eye.

"I told Burman the whole story. If you choose not to believe it, that's not my fault. But there may still be time. What's the situation in the city?"

"There is *no* time, Mr. Bayard. No time at all. . . ." To my

131

horror I saw a tear glisten at the corner of the thick man's eye.

"What . . ." I couldn't finish the question.

"The invaders have released a poisonous gas which has blanketed the city. They have erected barricades against any attempt at relief. Strange men in helmeted suits are shooting down every man who approaches . . ."

"But what about . . . the people . . . What about my wife? What—"

He was shaking his head. "The Emperor and his family, the government, everyone, all must be presumed dead, Mr. Bayard, inside the barricaded city!"

There was a shattering crash from the outer room. The thick man whirled from me, jumped to the door, shot a look out, then went through at a dead run, Burman at his heels. I yelled at Major Gunnarson to stop or I'd shoot, but he didn't and neither did I. There was a clatter of feet, a crash like breaking glass, a couple of shots. Someone yelled "The ape-men!" There were more shots, then a heavy slam like a body hitting the floor. I backed into the corner of my cell, cursing the fatal mistake I'd made in letting myself get cornered here. I aimed at the door, waited for the first Hagroon to come through—

The door flew open—and a familiar narrow-shouldered figure in stained whites sauntered into view.

"Dzok!" I yelled. "Get me out of here—or—" A horrible suspicion dawned. Dzok must have seen it in my face.

"Easy, old fellow!" He shouted as my gun covered him. "I'm here to give you a spot of assistance, old chap—and from the looks of things, you can jolly well use it!"

"What's going on out there?" I yelled. There was someone behind Dzok. A tall young fellow in a green coat and scarlet knee pants came through the door, holding a long-barrelled rifle with a short bayonet fixed to the end of it. There were white facings on the coat, wide loops of braid, and rows of bright gold buttons. There was a wide cocked hat on his head, with a gold fringe and a crimson rosette, and he wore white stockings and polished black shoes with large gilt buckles. The owner of the finery flashed me a big smile, then turned to Dzok and gave a sloppy salute with the palm of his hand out.

"I reckon we peppered 'em good, sor. Now what say ye we have a look about out back here for any more o' the gossoons as might be skulkin' ready to do in a honest man?"

"Never mind that, sergeant," Dzok said. "This is a jail delivery, nothing more. Those chaps out there are our allies, actually. Pity about the shooting, but it couldn't be helped." He was talking to me now. "I attempted to make a few inquiries, but found everyone in a state of the most extreme agitation. They opened fire with hardly a second glance, amid shouts of 'hairy ape-men'! Disgraceful——"

"The Hagroon have hit the capital," I cut him off. "Laid down a gas attack, barricaded the streets, everybody presumed dead...." I wasn't thinking now—just reacting. The Hagroon had to be stopped. That was all that mattered. Not that anything really mattered any more, with Barbro gone with the rest—but she was a fighter. She'd have expected me to go on fighting, too, as long as I could still move and breathe.

Dzok looked stricken. "Beastly, old fellow! I can't tell you how sorry I am..." He commiserated with me for awhile. Then the sergeant came back from the outer room with a key, opened my cell door.

"And so I came too late," Dzok said bitterly. "I had hoped..." He let the sentence trail off, as we went into the outer room.

"Who are these fellows?" I gaped at the half-dozen bright-plumaged soldiers posted about the jail covering the windows and the door.

"These are my volunteers, Bayard—my Napoleonic levies. I was on a recruiting mission, you'll recall. After I left you, I went back and loaded these chaps into my cargo shuttle, and returned to Zaj—and found—you'll never guess, old fellow!"

"I'll take three guesses," I said, "and they'll all be 'the Hagroon'."

Dzok nodded glumly. "The bounders had overrun Authority headquarters, including the Web terminal, of course. I beat a hasty strategic retreat, and followed your trail here..." he paused, looking embarrassed. "Actually, old chap, I'd hoped to enlist the aid of your Imperium. We Xonijeelians are ill-equipped to fight a Web war, I'm sorry to say. Always before——"

"I know. They caught us off-guard too. I wondered all along why you figured you were immune——"

"The audacity of the blighters! Who'd have expected——"

"You should have," I said shortly.

"Ah, well, what's done is done." Dzok rubbed his hands together with every appearance of relish. "Inasmuch as you're not in a position to assist me, perhaps my chaps and I can

133

still be of some help here. Better start by giving me a complete resumé of the situation. . . ."

After ten minutes' talk, while the troops kept up a sporadic fire from the jail windows, Dzok and I had decided on a plan of action. It wasn't a good one, but under the circumstances it was better than nothing. The first step was to find the S-suit. We wasted another ten minutes searching the place before I decided to try the vault. It was open, and the suit was laid out on a table.

"Right," Dzok said with satisfaction. "I'll need tools, Bayard, and a heat source and a magnifying glass. . . ."

We rummaged, found a complete tool kit in a wall locker and a glass in the chief's desk drawer. I made a hasty adaptation of a hot plate used for heating coffee, while Dzok opened up the control console set in the chest of the suit.

"We're treading on dangerous ground, of course," he said blandly, while he snipped hair-fine wires, teased them into new arrangements. "What I'm attempting is theoretically possible, but it's never been tried—not with an S-suit."

I watched, admiring the dexterity of his long grayish fingers as he rearranged the internal components of the incredibly compact installation. For half an hour, while guns cracked intermittently, he made tests, muttered, tried again, studying the readings on the miniature scales set on the cuff of the suit. Then he straightened, gave me a wry look.

"It's done, old chap. I can't guarantee the results of my makeshift mods, but there's at least an even chance that it will do what we want."

I asked for an explanation of what he had done, followed closely as he pointed out the interplay of circuits that placed stresses on the M-C field in such a way as to distort its normal function along a line of geometric progression leading to infinity . . .

"It's over my head, Dzok," I told him. "I was never a really first-class M-C man, and when it comes to your Xonijeelian complexities—"

"Don't trouble your head, Bayard. All you need to know is that adjusting this setting . . ." he pointed with a pin drill at a tiny knurled knob—"controls the angle of incidence of the pinch-field—"

"In plain English, if something goes wrong and I'm not dead, I can twiddle that and try again."

"Very succinctly put. Now let's be going. How far did you say it is to the city?"

134

"About twelve kilometers."

"Right. We'll have to commandeer a pair of light lorries. There are several parked in the court just outside. Some sort of crude steam-cars, I think—"

"Internal combustion. And not so crude; they'll do a hundred kilometers an hour."

"They'll serve." He went into the guard room, checked the scene from the windows.

"Quiet out there at the moment. No point in waiting about. Let's sally at once." I nodded, and Dzok gave his orders to the gaily costumed riflemen, five of whom quietly took up positions at the windows and door facing the courtyard, while the others formed up a cordon around Dzok and me.

"Hell, we may as well do our bit," I suggested. There were carbines in the gun locker. I took one, tossed one to Dzok, buckled on a belt and stuffed it with ammo.

"Tell your lads to shoot low," I said. "don't let anybody get in our way, but try not to kill anybody. They don't know what's going on out there—"

"And there's no time to explain," Dzok finished for me, looking at his men. "Shoot to wound, right, lads? Now, Sergeant, take three men and move out. Cover the first lorry and hold your fire until they start something. Mr. Bayard and I will come next, with ten men, while the rest of you lay down a covering fire. Those in the rear guard stand fast until number two lorry pulls up to the door, then pile in quickly and we're off."

"Very well, sor," the sergeant said. He was working hard on a plug of tobacco he'd found in the police chief's desk drawer. He turned and bawled instructions to his men, who nodded, grinning.

"These boys don't behave like recruits," I said. "They look like veterans to me."

Dzok nodded, smiling his incredible smile. "Former members of the Welsh regiment of the Imperial Guard. They were eager for a change."

"I wonder what you offered them?"

"The suggestion of action after a few months changing of the guard at Westminster was sufficient."

The sergeant was at the door now, with two of his men. He said a quick word, and the three darted out, sprinted for the lorry, a high-sided dark blue panel truck lettered FLOTTS-BRO POLIS. A scattering of shots rang out. Grass tips flew as a bullet clipped the turf by the sergeant's ankle. The man

135

on his left stumbled, went down, rolled, came up limping, his thigh wet with a dark glisten against the scarlet cloth. He made it in two jumps to the shelter of the truck, hit the grass, leveled his musket and fired. A moment later, all three were in position, their guns cracking in a one-round-per-second rhythm. The opposing fire slackened.

"Now," Dzok said. I brought the carbine up across my chest and dashed for the second truck. There was a white puff of smoke from a window overlooking the courtyard, a whine past my head. I ducked, pounded across the grass, leaped the chain at the edge of the pavement, skidded to a halt beside the lorry. Dzok was there ahead of me, wrenching at the door.

"Locked!" he called, and stepped back, fired a round into the keyhole, wrenched the door open. I caught a glimpse of his shuttle, a heavy passenger-carrying job, parked across a flowerbed. He followed my gaze.

"Just have to leave it. Too bad . . ." He was inside then, staring at the unfamiliar controls.

"Slide over!" I pushed in beside him, feeling the vehicle lurch as the men crowded in behind me, hearing the *spang!* as a shot hit the metal body. There were no keys in the ignition. I tried the starter; nothing.

"I'll have to short the wiring," I said, and slid to the ground, jumped to the hood, unlatched the wide side panel, lifted it. With one hard jerk, I twisted the ignition wires free, made hasty connections to the battery, then grabbed the starter lever and depressed it. The engine groaned, turned over twice, and caught with a roar. I slammed the hood down as a bullet cut a bright streak in it, jumped for the seat.

"Who's driving the second truck?"

"I have a chap who's a steam-car operator—

"No good. I'll have to start it for him. . . ." I was out again, running for the other lorry, parked twenty feet away. A worried-looking man with damp red hair plastered to a freckled forehead was fumbling with the dash lighter and headlight switch. There was a key in the switch of this one; I twisted it, jammed a foot against the starter. The engine caught, ran smoothly.

"You know how to shift gears?"

He nodded, smiling.

"This is the gas pedal. Push on it and you go faster. This is the brake . . ." He nodded eagerly. "If you stall out, push this floor button. The rest is just steering."

136

He nodded again as glass smashed in front of him, throwing splinters in our faces. Blood ran from a cut across his cheek, but he brushed the chips away, gave me a wave. I ran for it, reached my truck, slammed it in gear, watched a moment to see that the redhead picked up the rear guard. Then I gunned for the closed iron gates, hit them with a crash at twenty miles an hour, slammed through, twisted the wheel hard left, and thundered away down the narrow street.

It took us twenty minutes to cover the twelve kilometers to the edge of the city. For the last hundred yards, we slowed, steered a course among bodies lying in the street, pulled up at a rough barricade of automobiles turned on their sides and blackened by fire, bright tongues of flame still licking over the smouldering tires. A church tower clock was tolling midnight—a merry sound to accompany the cheery picture.

I looked at the dark towers of the city behind the barrier, the dark streets. There were at least a dozen men in sight, sprawled in the unlovely attitudes of violent death. None was in uniform or armed; they were bystanders, caught in the clouds of poison that had rolled out from the city's streets. There were no Hagroon in sight. The streets were as still as a graveyard.

There was a sound to the left. I brought my carbine up, saw a hatless man in a white shirt.

"Thank God you've got here at last," he choked. "I got a whiff—sick as a dog. Pulled a couple back, but..." he coughed, retched, bending double. "Too late. All dead. Gas is gone now, blown away..."

"Get farther back," I said. "Spread the word not to try to attack the barricades." There was another man behind him, and a woman, her face soot-streaked.

"What do you want us to do?" someone called. They clustered around the car, a dozen battered survivors, thinking we were the police, and ready to do whatever had to be done to help us.

"Just stay back, keep out of harms' way. We're going to try something—"

Someone yelled then, pointing at Dzok. A cry went through the crowd.

"Everybody out—fast!" I barked to the men in the rear of the truck. Then: "This is a friend!" I yelled to the crowd. I jumped down, ran around to the side where the man had

137

raised the first outcry, caught him by the arm as he jerked at the shattered door handle.

"Listen to me! This isn't the enemy! He's an ally of the Imperium! He's here to help! These are his troops!" I waved at the ten costumed soldiers who had formed a rough circle around the truck. The headlights of the second truck swung into view then. It growled up beside the first, chugged to a stop and stalled out. The doors flew open and men swarmed out.

"He's got hair on his face—just like the others—"

"You saw them?"

"No—but I heard—from the man I pulled back from the barricade—before he died—"

"Well, I don't have hair on my face—unless you want to count three day's beard. This is Commander Dzok! He's on our side. Now, spread the word! I don't want any accidents!"

"Who're you?"

"I'm Colonel Bayard, Imperial Intelligence. I'm here to do what I can—"

"What can we do?" several voices called. I repeated my instructions to stay back.

"What about you?" the man who had spotted Dzok asked me. "What's your plan, Colonel?"

Dzok was out of the car now. He handed the modified S-suit to me, turned and bowed in courtly fashion to the crowd.

"Enchanted, sirs and madams, to make your acquaintance," he called. Someone tittered, but Dzok ignored it. "I have the honor, as Colonel Bayard has said, to offer my services in the fight against the rude invader. But it is the Colonel himself who must carry out our mission here tonight. The rest of us can merely assist . . ."

"What's he going to do?"

I had the suit halfway on now. Dzok was helping me, pulling it up, getting my arms into the sleeves, settling the heavy chest pack in place, zipping long zippers closed.

"Using this special equipment," Dzok said in his best theatrical manner, "Colonel Bayard will carry out a mission of the utmost peril . . ."

"Skip the pitch and hand me the helmet," I interrupted him.

"We want to help," someone called.

"I'd like to go along," another voice said.

"Our chief need at the moment," Dzok's voice rang above the rest, "is a supply of-coffee. My brave lads are a trifle

138

fatigued, not having rested since leaving their home barracks. For the rest, we can only wait—"

"Why can't some of us go along, Colonel," a man said, stepping close. "You could use an escort—and not those overdressed fancy dans, either!"

"The Colonel must go alone," Dzok said. "Alone he will carry out a spy mission among the enemy—on the other side of time!" He turned to me, and in a lower voice said: "Don't waste any time, old fellow. It's after midnight now—in about two hours the world ends. . . ."

The transparent helmet was in place, all the contacts tight. Dzok made a couple of quick checks, gave me the O sign with his fingers that meant all systems were go. I put my hand on the "activate" button and took my usual deep breath. If Dzok's practice was as good as his theory, the rewired S-suit would twist the fabric of reality in a different manner than its designers had intended, stress the E-field of the normal continuum in a way that would expel me, like a watermelon seed squeezed in the fingers, into that curious non-temporal state of null entropy—the other side of time, as he poetically called it.

If it worked, that was. And there was only one way to find out. I pressed the button—

CHAPTER FOURTEEN

There was a moment of total vertigo; the world inverted itself around me, dwindled to a pinhole through which all reality flowed, to expand vastly, whirling . . .

I was standing in the street, looking across at the black hulks of burned-out cars glowing with a bluish light like corpses nine days under water. I turned, saw the empty police lorries, the dead bodies in the street, the stark, leafless trees lining the avenue, the blank eyes of the houses behind them. Dzok, the soldiers, the crowd—all of them had vanished in the instant that the suit's field had sprung into being—or, more correctly, I had vanished from among them. Now I was alone, in the same deserted city I had seen when I awakened after my inexplicable encounter with the flaming man in the basement of Imperial Intelligence Headquarters.

I looked again at the clock on the church tower: the hands stood frozen at twelve twenty-five. And the clock I had seen in the office just after the encounter had read twelve-o-five. I was already too late to intercept the flaming man before he did whatever he had been there to accomplish.

But I wasn't too late to spy out the Hagroon position, discover where the discontinuity engine was planted, then return, lead an assault force ...

There were too many variables in the situation. Action was the only cure for the hollow sensation of foredoomed failure growing in the pit of my stomach.

A pebble hopped suddenly, struck the toe of my shoe as I took a step. Small dust clouds rose, swirled toward my feet as I crossed the dry, crumbling soil where grass had grown only moments before. The eerie light that seemed to emanate from the ground showed me a pattern of depressions in the soil that seemed to form before my foot reached them. ...

I looked behind me. There were no prints to show where I had come, but a faint trail seemed to lead ahead. A curious condition, this null time. ...

I crossed the sidewalk, skirted a dead man lying almost on the barricade. I clambered over the burned wreck of a car, a boxy sedan with an immense spare tire strapped to the rear. There were more bodies on the other side—men who had died trying to climb the wall, or who had chosen that spot to make a stand. Among them a lone Hagroon lay, the bulky body contorted in the heavy atmosphere suit, a bloody hole in the center of his chest. Someone on the Imperial side had drawn enemy blood. The thought was cheering in this scene of desolation. I went on, glanced up at the tower clock as I passed—

The hands stood at one minute after twelve. As I watched, the minute hand jerked back, pointed straight up.

And suddenly I understood. Dzok's changes to the S-suit had had the desired effect of shifting me to null time. But both of us had forgotten the earlier adjustment he had made to the suit's controls—the adjustment that had caused the suit to carry me in a retrograde direction, back along the temporal profile, during my trip from the jungle world. Now, with the suit activated, holding me in my unnatural state of anti-entropy, the retrograde motion had resumed. I was traveling backward through time!

I walked on, watching the curious behavior of objects as they impinged on the E-field of the suit, or crossed from the field to the external environment. A pebble kicked by me took up a motion, flew from the field—where it resumed its natural temporal direction, sprang back, seemed to strike my foot, then dropped from play. The air around me whispered in constant turmoil as vagrant currents were caught, displaced backward in time, only to be released, with the resultant local inequalities in air pressure. I wondered how I would appear to an outside observer—or if I could be seen at all. And my weapon; what effect would—or *could* it have, fired in the future, dealing death in the past—

Soundlessly, a figure backed into view around a corner two blocks away, walked briskly toward me, the feet moving back, the arms swinging—like a movie run in reverse. I flattened myself against a wall, watched as the walker came closer. A Hagroon! I felt my hackles rise. I flipped the slug gun into my hand, waited . . .

He stepped past me, kept going, his head turning as though scanning the sidewalk for signs of life—but he paid no attention to me. I looked around. There were none of his fellows in sight. It was as good a time as any to make a test. I stepped boldly out, aimed the gun at his retreating chest at a distance of twenty feet, twenty-five . . .

There was no reaction. I was invisible to him, while he, somehow, remained visible to me. I could only assume that light rays striking me were affected by the field, their temporal progression reversed, with the effect of simply blanking them off, while normal light emanating from the scene to me . . .

But how could I see, with light traveling *away* from my eyes. . . .

I remembered a statement made by an Imperium Net physicist, explaining why it was possible to scan the continua through which a moving shuttle passed in an immeasurably short instant of time: "Light is a condition, not an event. . . ."

Whatever the reason, the Hagroon couldn't see me. A break for our side at last. Now to see what I could accomplish on the strength of one small advantage and whatever luck I could find along the way.

It was half an hour's walk to the Net Garages. There were few corpses in the street along the way. Apparently the people had been caught in their beds by the attack. Those few who had been abroad had fallen back toward the barricades—and died there. I passed a pair of Hagroon, walking briskly backward, then a group of a half dozen, then a column of twenty or thirty, all moving in the opposite direction from my own course, which meant that, in normal progression, they were headed for the area of the Net Garages, coming from the direction of the Imperial HQ.

Two blocks from there, the crowd of Hagroon almost filled the street.

Moving with the stream—which seemed to part before me, to the accompaniment of perplexed looks on the Hagroon faces I glimpsed through the dark faceplates—I made my way across the North Bridge, through the dim-glowing wrought-iron gates before the looming bulk of the headquarters building. The mob of Hagroon here was tight-packed, a shoving, sullen mass of near-humanity—jostling their way backward through the wide doors, overflowing the gravel walks and the barren rectangles of dry dirt that were immaculately manicured flower beds in normal times. I caught a glimpse of a clock in the front of a building across the plaza—eleven fifteen.

I had moved back through time three-quarters of an hour, while thirty subjective minutes passed.

I made my way through the streaming crowd of suited Hagroon, reached the door, slipped through into the same high-ceilinged foyer that I had left, alone, six weeks earlier. Now it was crowded with silent Hagroon masses, overseen by two heavily brassed individuals who stood on the lower steps of the flight leading to the upper floors, waving their arms and grimacing. Sound, it appeared, failed to span the interface between "normal" null time and my reversed field effect.

The stream pressed toward a side corridor. I made my way there, reached a small door set in the hall with the sign SERVICE STAIR beside it—

I remembered that door. It was the one through which I had pursued the flaming man, so many weeks before. I pushed through it, felt the ghostly jostle of Hagroon bodies that seemed to slip aside an instant before I touched them, descended one flight, followed the direction of the stream of aliens along to a door—the one beyond which the fiery man had turned at bay. . . .

The stream of Hagroon was smaller now, less tightly packed. I stood aside, watched as the creatures shuffled backward through the narrow entry into the small room— and more and more, packing into the confined space. . . .

It wasn't possible. I had seen hundreds of the brutes in the streets, packing the entryway, crowding the corridors, all streaming here—or *from* here in the normal time sequence— from this one small room. . . .

There were only a few Hagroon in the hall now, standing listening to a silent harangue from a brass-spangled officer. They shuffled back, almost eagerly passed into the room. The officers appeared from above, joined in a brief huddle, backed through the door into the gloom. I followed—and stopped dead.

A glistening, ten-foot disk of insubstantiality shimmered in the air, floating an inch or two above the dull stone floor, not quite grazing the dusty beamed ceiling of the abandoned storeroom. As I watched, one of the remaining Hagroon officers backed quickly to it, crouched slightly, leaped backward through the disk—and disappeared as magically as a rabbit into a magician's hat. There were only two Hagroon left now. One of them backed to the disk, hopped through. The last spoke into a small hand-held instrument, stood for a moment gazing about the room, ignoring me utterly. Then he too sprang through the disk and was gone.

I was seeing wonders, which, by comparison, the shuttles of the Imperium were as prosaic as wicker baby buggies, but there was no time to stand in awe, gaping. This was an entry portal from some other space to null-time Stockholm. The Hagroon had entered through it; from where, I didn't know. There was a simple empirical method of answering that question. . . .

I went to the disk—like the surface of a rippled pond, upended in gloom. There was nothing visible beyond that mysterious plane. I gritted my teeth, took an instant to hope I was guessing right, and stepped through.

I knew at once that I was back in normal time—still running backwards, doubtless, still in the same room—but I was standing in honest darkness, away from the pervasive death light of null time. There were Hagroon all about me, bulky, suited figures, almost filling the confined space of the room, overflowing into the corridor, seemingly unbothered by the lack of illumination. I recognized the officers I had seen moments before, the last to pass through the portals—or the first, in normal time: the pioneers sent through ahead of the main body to reconnoiter—before the horde poured through, to stream back to the Net Garages. Six weeks earlier —or tonight; either way of looking at it was equally valid— I would meet them there, embarking in their shuttles to return to the Hagroon world line, their job here finished. But now, because of the miracle of my retrograde motion in the time stream, I was seeing the play acted out in reverse; watching the victorious troops, flushed from their victory over the sleeping city, about to back out into the streets, and re-enact their gas attack.

Many of the Hagroon, I noted, carried heavy canisters. Others, as I watched, took empty containers from a heap in the corridor, hitched them into place on their backs. They were filing away now, by two's and three's, backing out into the corridors, up the stairs, back into the dead streets. I started to follow—then checked myself. There was something tugging at the edge of my awareness. Something I must do, now—quickly—before my chance slipped away. Events were flowing inexorably toward their inevitable conclusion, while I hesitated, racking my brain. It was hard to think, hard to orient my thoughts in the distorted perspective of reversed time; but I had to stop now, force myself to analyze what I was seeing, reconstruct the attack.

The Hagroon had arrived at the Net Garages. I had seen their shuttles there. It was the perfect spot for an assault in force via shuttle, and due to the characteristic emanations of the Net communicator carriers, easy to pinpoint for navigation purposes.

Once there, they had marched across the empty null-time city to Intelligence Headquarters, a convenient central location from which to attack, and with plenty of dark cellar rooms— and perhaps there was also an element of sardonic humor in their choice of staging areas....

Then the troops had poured through the portal, emerged into the midnight streets of the real-time city, spewing gas— the attack the end of which I was now witnessing.

Then they had returned through the portal, crossed to their shuttles again in null time—the exodus I had just witnessed....

But why the gas attack on a city about to suffer annihilation along with the rest of the planet?

Simple: The Hagroon needed peace and quiet in which to erect the discontinuity engine—and they needed the assurance that the infernal machine would remain undisturbed for the necessary time to allow them to pass back through their portal into null time, regain their shuttles, and leave the doomed A-line. By gassing the city, they had ensured their tranquillity while they perpetrated the murder of a universe.

Because it was more than a world they killed. It was a planet, a solar system, a sky filled with stars, to the ends of conceivable space and beyond—a unique, irreplaceable aspect of reality, to be wiped forever from the face of the continuum, because one world, one tiny dust-mote in that universe posed a possible threat to Hagroon safety. It was an abominable plot—and the moments during which I could take action to

144

thwart it were fast slipping away. Somewhere, at this moment, a crew was at work, preparing the doomsday device. And if I delayed, even for minutes, in finding it—it would be too late or (too early!). The machine would be separated into its component parts, carried away to the shuttles by backward-walking men, transported out of range—

I had to find the engine—now!

I looked around. Hagroon laden with empty canisters were still backing away along the corridor. Their officers waved their arms, mouths moving behind faceplates. One individual, helmetless, caught my attention. He came from the opposite direction along the narrow hall, stepping briskly up to the Hagroon directing the canister operation. Two rank-and-file Hagroon preceded him. They turned away, joined a group plucking empty canisters from a heap and fitting them on their backs. The helmetless one talked to the officer; both nodded, talked some more; then the former backed away down the dark hall—away from the stair. I hesitated a moment, then followed.

He backed off fifty feet, turned into a storeroom much like the one in which the portal had been erected. There were four other Hagroon there, crouching around a heavy tripod on which a massive construction rested, its casing lying on the floor to one side.

Luck was with me. I had found the discontinuity engine.

The next step was clear to me in the same instant that I saw the engine. As two of the Hagroon paused, staring with comically puzzled expressions, I went to the stand, planted my feet, gripped the massive casing, and lifted. It came away easily. My slightly accelerated time rate, although reversed, gave me an added quota of brute strength. I stepped back, hugging the horror device to my chest, feeling the buzz of its timer—and to my blank amazement, saw it still resting where it had been—while I held its counterpart in my hands. The Hagroon technicians were working away, apparently undisturbed. But then, I hadn't yet appeared, to create paradox before their startled eyes. . . .

I turned to the door, made my way along the corridor, climbed the steps, set off at the fastest dog trot I could manage for the Net Garages.

I made it in twenty minutes, in spite of the awkward burden, forcing myself to ignore the gas attack going on all

145

around me. Suited Hagroon clumped backward through the well-lit streets under a vague cloud of brownish gas that seemed to slowly coalesce, drawing together as I watched. I half-ran, half-walked, shifting my grip on the heavy casing, sweating heavily now inside the suit. The gas was all around me, and I hoped the seals of my garment were as secure as Dzok had assured me they were.

At the garages, a few morose-looking Hagroon loitered about the parked shuttles, peering out through the wide doors toward the sounds of action in the city streets. I passed them unnoticed, went to the last shuttle in line—the same machine I had ridden once before. I knew it had preset controls, which would automatically home it on its A-line of origin—the Hagroon world. I pulled open the door, lowered my burden to the grey metal floor, pushed it well inside, then checked the wall clock. Dzok and I had calculated that the engine had gone into action at two A.M. precisely. It was now ten forty-five; three hours and fifteen minutes until M minute.

And the transit of the shuttle from the Zero-zero line to the Hagroon line had taken three hours and twenty-five minutes.

I had ten minutes to kill. . . .

The discontinuity engine was already counting down toward its moment of cataclysmic activity—the titanic outpouring of energy which would release the stasis which constituted the fabric of reality for this line of alternate existence. I had plucked it from the hands of its makers just as they were completing their installation. When the time came, it would perform. The shuttle was the problem now. I climbed inside, looked over the controls. They, at least, were simple enough. A trip wire, attached to the main field switch . . .

I went back out, found a length of piano wire on a workbench at one side of the garage, secured it to the white painted lever that controlled the shuttle's generators, led the wire out through the door. Five minutes to go, now. It was important to get the timing as exact as possible. I watched the hands of the clock move back: ten thirty-four; ten thirty-three; ten thirty-two; ten thirty-one. There was a faint vibration from the shuttle. . . .

I closed the door carefully, checked to be sure the wire was clear, then gripped it, gave it a firm pull. The shuttle seemed to waver. It shimmered, winked for an instant—then sat, solid and secure, unmoving. I let out a breath; the example of the engine had forewarned me. The results of my actions on

146

external objects weren't visible to me, but I had sent the shuttle on its way. This was its past reality I saw before me now.

CHAPTER FIFTEEN

Back in the street, the attack was in full swing. I saw a man lying in the gutter rise, like a dummy on a rope, clutch at his throat, run backwards into a building—a corpse risen from the dead. The brown cloud hung low over the pavement now, a flat stratum of deadly gas. A long plume formed, flowed toward a Hagroon, whipped into the end of the hand-held horn of his dispenser. Other plumes shaped up, flowed toward other attackers. I was watching the gas attack in reverse—the killers, scavenging the streets of the poison that would decimate the population. I followed them as the poisonous cloud above gathered, broke apart, flowed back into the canisters from which it had come. I saw the invaders, laden now, slogging in their strange reverse gait back toward the dark bulk of Intelligence HQ. And I followed, crowding with them along the walk, through the doors, along the corridor, down the narrow steps, back to the deserted storeroom where they poured in a nightmare stream through the shining disk, back to null time and their waiting shuttles.

There was a paralyzing choice of courses of action open to me now—and my choice had to be the right one—with the life of a universe the cost of an error.

The last of the Hagroon passed through the portal, returning to null time, to march back to the Net Garages, board their shuttles and disappear back toward their horrendous home world. The portal stood deserted in the empty room, in a silence as absolute as deafness. I stood by it, waiting, as minutes ticked past—minutes of subjective time, during which I moved inexorably back, back—to the moment when the Hagroon had first activated the portal—and I saw it dwindle abruptly, shrink to a point of incredible brilliance, wink out.

I blinked my eyes against the darkness, then switched on a small lamp set in the suit's chest panel, intended as an aid in map and instrument reading during transit through lightless continua. It served to show me the dim outlines of the room, the dusty packing cases, the littered floor—nothing else. The portal, I was now certain, required no focusing device to establish its circle of congruency between null and real time.

I waited a quarter of an hour to allow time for the Hagroon to leave the vicinity of the portal, studying my wrist controls and reviewing Dzok's instructions. Then I twisted the knob that would thrust me back through the barrier to null time. I felt the universe turn inside out while the walls whirled around me; then I was standing in null time, alone, breathing hard, but all right so far.

I looked around, and saw what I was looking for—a small, dull metal case, perched on a stand, half-obscured behind a stack of cases—the portal machine. I went to it, put a hand on it. It was humming gently, idling, ready to serve its monstrous owners when they arrived, minutes from now in normal time.

There were tools in a leather case clipped to the arm of my suit. I took out a screwdriver, removed the screws. The top of the case came off, showed me a maze of half-familiar components. I studied the circuits, recognized an analog of the miniature moebius-wound coil that formed the heart of my S-suit. The germ of an idea was taking shape—a trick probably impossible, certainly difficult, and very likely impractical, even if I had the necessary technical knowledge to carry it out—but an idea of such satisfying scope that I found myself smiling down in Satanic anticipation at the machine in my hands. Dzok had told me a little about the working of the S-suit—and I had watched as he had modified the circuits on two occasions. Now it was my turn to try. If I could bring it off . . .

Twenty minutes later I had done what I could. It was simple enough in theory. The focusing of the portal was controlled by a simple nuclear-force capacitor, tuned by a cyclic gravitational field. By reversing contacts, as Dzok had done when adjusting the suit to carry me backward in time as I crossed the continua, I had modified the orientation of the lens effect. Now, instead of establishing congruency at a level of temporal parity, the portal would set up a contact with a level of time in the future—perhaps as much as a week or two. I could go back now, reverse the action of the suit, and give my warning. With two weeks or more to convince Imperial Intelligence that I was something other than a madman with a disturbing likeness to one B. Bayard, I could surely make them see reason. True, there would be a number of

148

small problems, such as the simultaneous existence of two battered ex-diplomats of that name—but that was a minor point, if I could avert the total destruction that waited in the wings.

I replaced the cover, for the first time feeling a throb of hope that my mad gamble could pay off—that in moving back through time to a point before the Hagroon attack, I might actually have changed the course of coming events. If I was right, it meant that the invaders I had seen pouring through the portal would never come—had never come; that the gas attack was relegated to the realm of unrealized possibilities; and that the city's inhabitants sleeping peacefully now would wake in the morning, unaware of the death they had died and risen from. . . .

It was a spooky thought. I had done what I could here. Now it was time to go. I braced my stomach against the wrench of the S-suit's null-time field, reversed the control. . . .

I blinked, letting my senses swim back into focus. I was back in real time, in the dark, deserted storeroom. There was no sign of the portal—and now, if my guesses were right, there wouldn't be for many days—and then the startled Hagroon would emerge into a withering fire from waiting Imperial troops.

Back in the hall, I licked my lips, suddenly as dry as a mummy's. The next step was one I didn't like. Tampering with my suit was dangerous business, and I'd had my share of daring experimentation for the night. But it had to be done.

The light here was dim—too dim for fine work. I went up the stairs to the ground floor corridor, saw a group of men back across the entry hall, walk backwards up the stairs that led to the second floor. I stifled the impulse to rush out with glad cries; they wouldn't hear me. They were as impervious to sounds coming from the past as the Hagroon. I was a phantom, moving in an unreal world of living memories, unreeled in reverse like a glimpse of an old album, riffled through from back to front. And when I had reversed the action of the S-suit, I'd still have the problem of making someone believe me.

It was hard, admittedly, for anyone to take my story seriously when my double—another me—was available to deny my authenticity. And nothing would have changed. I—the "I" of six weeks ago, minus the scars I had collected since then, was at home—now—dining in my sumptuous villa, with the incomparable Barbro, about to receive a mysterious

149

phone call—and I would appear—a dirt-streaked man in torn clothing of outlandish cut, needing a shave and a bath, and talking nonsense. But this time at least I'd have a few days to convince them.

I stepped back into the cross corridor, found an empty office, closed and locked the door and turned on the light. Then, without waiting to consider the consequences of a miscalculation, I switched off the suit's power-pack. I unzipped, lifted the light helmet off, pulled the suit off, looked around the room. Everything seemed normal. I reached to the desk, gingerly lifted the black-handled paper knife that lay there—and with a sinking sensation saw it, still lying on the desk—the duplicate of the one in my hand. I tossed the knife back to the desk—and it winked out of existence—gone along the stream of normal time.

It was what I had been afraid of: even with the suit off, I was still living backwards.

Again, I got out the miniature tool kit, used it to open the chest control pack. I knew which wires to reverse. With infinite care, I shifted the hair-fine filaments into new positions, guessing, when my recollection of Dzok's work failed. If I had known I'd be doing this job alone, I could have had Dzok run through it with me, even made notes. But both of us, in the excitement of the moment, had forgotten that I would slide away into past time as soon as the suit was activated. Now he was out of reach, hours in the future.

I finished at last, with a splitting headache, and a taste in my mouth like an abandoned rat's nest. My empty stomach simultaneously screeched for food and threatened violence if I so much as thought about the subject. I had been operating for the best part of forty-eight hours now without food, drink, or rest.

I pulled the suit back on, zipped up, too tired now even to worry, flipped the control—and knew at once that something was wrong—badly wrong.

It wasn't the usual nauseous wrench that I had come to expect; just a claustrophobic sense of pressure and heat. There was a loud humming in my ears, and a cloying in my throat as I drew a breath of scalding air.

I stepped to the desk, my legs as sluggish as lead castings. I picked up the paperweight—strangely heavy—

It was hot! I dropped it, watched it slam to the desk top. I dragged in another breath—with a sensation of drowning. The air was as thick as water, hot as live steam . . .

I exhaled a frosty plume of ice crystals. The sleeve of the suit caught my eye. It was glazed over with a dull white coating. I touched it with a finger, felt the heat of it, the slickness. It was ice—hot ice, forming on my suit! Even as I watched, it thickened, coating my sleeve, building up on my faceplate. I bent my arm to wipe it clear, saw crusts break, leap toward the floor with frantic speed. I managed to get one finger-swipe across the plastic visor. Through the clear strip, I saw a mirror across the room. I started for it—my legs strained uselessly. I was rooted to the spot, enchased in ice as rigid as armor!

My faceplate was frosted over solidly now. I tried to move an arm; it was rigid too. And suddenly, I understood. My tinkering with the suit's circuits had been less than perfect. I had re-established my normal direction of temporal progression—but my entropic rate was only a fraction of normal. I was an ice statue—an interesting find for the owner of the office when he broke the door down in the morning, unless I could break free fast!

I tensed my legs, threw my weight sideways—and felt myself toppling, whipping over to slam stunningly against the floor. My ice-armor smashed as I hit, and I moved quickly, brought one numbed arm up, groped for the control knob, fumbled at it with half-frozen fingers, twisted—

There was a sudden release of pressure. The faceplate cleared, dotted over with water droplets that bubbled, danced, disappeared. A blinding cloud was boiling up from me as the ice melted, flashed away as steam. I thrust against the floor, felt myself bound clear, rise halfway to the ceiling, then fall back as leisurely as an inflated balloon. I landed on one leg, felt the pressure build as the ankle twisted. I got my other foot under me, staggered, regained my balance, cursing between clenched teeth at the agony in the strained joint. I grabbed for the control, fumbled over the cold surface—

The control knob was gone. The twist I had given with numbed fingers had broken it off short!

I limped to the door, caught the knob, twisted—

The metal tore; pain shot through my hand. I looked at my palm, saw ripped skin. I had the strength of a Gargantua without the toughness of hide to handle it. I had overcontrolled. Now my entropic rate was double or triple the normal one. My body heat was enough to boil water. The friction of

151

my touch bubbled paint! Carefully I twisted the door's lock, pulled at the crushed knob. The door moved sluggishly, heavy as a vault. I pushed past it into the hall—and lurched to a stop.

A seven-foot specimen of the Hagroon species stood glowering from a dark doorway ten feet across the corridor.

I backed away, flattened myself against the wall. This boy was a factor I hadn't counted on. He was a scout, probably, sent through hours ahead of the main column. I had seen the last of his fellows leave, and watched the portal blink out. On the strength of that, I had assumed they were all gone. But if the portal had been activated briefly, an hour earlier, as a test ...

Another academic question. He was here, as big as a grizzly and twice as ugly, a broad, thick troll in a baggy atmosphere suit, raising an arm slowly, putting a foot forward, heading my way—

I jumped aside, almost fell, as the Hagroon slammed heavily against the wall where I'd been standing—a wall charred black by the heat of my body. I moved back again, carefully this time. I had the speed on him, but if he caught me in that bonecrusher grip ...

He was mad—and scared. It showed in the snarling expression I could dimly see through the dark faceplate. Maybe he'd already been down to the portal room, and found his escape hatch missing. Or maybe the follow-up invasion force was behind schedule now. ...

I felt my heart take a sudden leap as I realized that I'd succeeded. I had worked over the suit for an hour, and perhaps another half-hour had gone by while I floundered in my slow-time state, building up a personal icecap—and they hadn't appeared on the scene. I could answer the theorists on one point now: a visitor to the past *could* modify the already-seen future, eliminate it from existence!

But the Hagroon before me was unaware of the highly abnormal aspects of his presence here. He was a fighter, trained to catch small hairless anthropos and squeeze their necks, and I fitted the description. He jumped again—a curiously graceless, slow-motion leap—hit and skidded, whirling ponderously to grab again—

I misjudged my distance, felt his hand catch at my sleeve. He was fast, this hulking monster. I pulled away, tore free—and stumbled as I skidded back, felt my feet go out from under me—

He was after me, while I flailed the air helplessly. One huge hand caught my arm, hauled me in, gathered me to his vast bosom. I felt the crushing pressure, almost heard the creak of my ribs as blood rushed blindingly to my face—

The fabric of his suit was bubbling, curling, blackening. His grip relaxed. I saw his face, his mouth open, and distantly, through his helmet and mine, I heard his scream of agony. His hands came up, fingers outspread, blistered raw by the terrible heat of my body. Even so, he ripped with them at his suit, tearing the molten plastic from his shaggy chest, exposing a bleeding second degree burn from chin to navel.

I continued my fall, took the shock on my outstretched hands, felt the floor come up and grind against my chin, felt the skin break, the spatter of hot blood. Then there was only the blaze of stars and a soft bottomless blackness. . . .

I lay on my back, feeling an Arctic chill that gripped my chest like a cold iron vise. I drew a wheezing breath, pressed my hands against the floor. They were numb, as dead as a pair of iceman's tongs, but I managed to get my feet under me, stagger upright. There were blackened footprints burned against the polished wood of the floor, and a larger black area where I had lain—and even as I burned the surfaces I touched, they bled away my heat, freezing me.

The Hagroon was gone. I saw a bloody hand-print on the wall, another farther along. He had headed for the service stair, bound no doubt for the storage room where the portal had been. He'd have a long wait. . . .

I leaned against the wall, racked with shivering, my teeth clamped together like a corpse in rigor. I had had enough of lone world-saving missions. It was time for someone else to join the party, share the honor—and incidentally, perform a delicate operation on my malfunctioning S-suit before I froze solid, fell on my face, and burned my way through to the basement.

I turned toward the front hall with a vague idea of finding someone—Richthofen, maybe. He was here tonight. Sure, good old Manfred, sitting at his desk upstairs, giving the third degree to a poor slob named Bayard, hauled on the carpet because some other poor slob of the same name was in jail a few miles away, claiming he was Bayard, and that the end of the world was nigh!

I reached the corner, staggered, feeling the hot flush of fever burning my face, while the strength drained from my legs, sucked away by the terrible entropic gradient between my runaway E-field and the normal space around me.

Bad stuff, Mr. B, tinkering with machines you don't understand. Machines made by a tribe of smart monkey-men who regard us sapiens as little better than homicidal maniacs—and with good reason, good reason . . .

I had fallen, and was on hands and knees watching the smoke curl up from between my numbed fingers. It was funny, that. Worth a laugh in anybody's joke book. I clawed at the wall, bubbling paint, got to my feet, made another yard toward the stair. . . .

Poor old Bayard; me. What a surprise he'd get, if he walked into that little room down below, and encountered one frightened, burned, murder-filled Hagroon—a pathetic leftover from a so-carefully-planned operation that had gotten itself lost along the way because it had overlooked a couple of small factors. The Hagroon, self-styled tough guys. Ha! They didn't know what real bloodthirstiness was until they ran up against good old Homo sap. Poor little monsters, they didn't have a chance . . .

Down again, and a mouthful of blood. Must have hit harder that time, square on the face. A good thing, maybe. Helps to clear the head. Where was I going? Oh, yes. Had to go along and warn poor old B. Can't let the poor fellow walk in all unsuspecting. Have to get there first . . . still have the slug gun . . . finish off bogie man. . . .

I was dimly aware of a door resisting as I leaned against it, then swinging wide, and I was falling, tumbling down stairs, bouncing, head over heels, slow and easy like a pillow falling—a final slam against the gritty, icy floor, the weight, and the pain. . . .

A long trip this. Getting up again, feeling the cold coming up the legs now like slow poison . . . cloud of brown gas, spreading up the legs, across the city. Have to warn them, tell them . . .

But they don't believe. Fools. Don't believe. God, how it hurts, and the long dark corridor stretching away, and the light swelling and fading, swelling again—

There he is! God, what a monster. Poor monster, hurt, crouched in the corner, rocking and moaning. Brought it on himself, the gas-spreading son of a bearskin rug! Sees me now, scrambling up. And look at those teeth! Makes old Dzok look like a grass-eater. Coming at me now. Get the gun out, feel it slap the palm, hold it, squeeze—

The gun was falling from my numbed hand, skidding on the floor, and I was groping for it, feeling with hands like stumps, seeing the big shape looming over me—

To hell with the gun. Can't press the firing stud anyway. Speed, that's all you've got now, m' lad. Hit him low, let his weight do the job, use your opponent's strength against him, judo in only five easy lessons, class starts Monday—

A blow like a runaway beer truck and I was skidding across the floor, and even through the suit I heard the sickening *crunch!* as the massive skull of the Hagroon struck the corner of a steel case, the ponderous *slam!* as he piled against the floor. I was on hands and knees again, not feeling the floor anymore, not feeling anything—just get on your feet once more and make sure . . .

I pulled myself up with the help of a big box placed conveniently beside me, took three wavering steps, bent over him. I saw the smear of blood, the thin ooze of fluid from the gaping wound above the ear, the black-red staining the inside of the helmet. Okay, Mr. Hagroon. You put up a good scrap, but that low block and lady luck were too much for you, and now—

I heard a noise from the door. There was a man there, dim in the wavering light of fading consciousness. I leaned, peering, with a strange sense of *déjà vu*, the seen-before . . .

He came toward me in slow-motion, and I blinked, wiped my hand across the steamed-over faceplate. He was in midair, in a dream leap, hands reaching for me. I checked myself, tried to back away, my hand outflung as though to hold back some unspeakable fate—

Long, pink sparks crackled from his hand to mine as he hung like a diver suspended in midair. I heard a noise like fat frying, and for one unbelievable instant glimpsed the face before me—

Then a silent explosion turned the world to blinding white, hurling me into nothingness.

CHAPTER SIXTEEN

It was a wonderful bed, wide and cool and clean, and the dream was wonderful too. Barbro's face, perfect as an artist's conception of the goddess of the hunt, framed by her dark red hair in a swirl of silken light. Just behind the rosy vision there were a lot of dark thoughts clamoring to be dragged out and reviewed, but I wasn't going to get hooked on that one. No sir, the good old dream was good enough for me, if only it wouldn't go away and leave me remembering dark shapes that moved in foul tunnels—and pain, and loss, the sickness of failure and dying hope—

The dream leaned closer and there were bright tears in the smoke-grey eyes, but the mouth was smiling, and then it was against mine, and I was kissing warm, soft lips—real lips, not the dream kind that always elude you. I raised a hand, felt a weight like an anvil stir, saw a vast bundle of white bandage swim into view.

"Barbro!" I said, and heard my voice emerge as a croak.

"Manfred! He's awake! He knows me!"

"Ah, a man would have to be far gone indeed to fail to know you, my dear," a cool voice said. Another face appeared, less pretty than the other, but a good face all the same. Baron von Richthofen smiled down at me, looking concerned and excited at the same time.

"Brion, Brion! What happened?" Barbro's cool fingertips touched my face. "When you didn't come home, I called, and Manfred told me you'd gone—and then they searched the building, and found footprints, burned—"

"Perhaps you'd better not press him now," Manfred murmured.

"No, of course not." A hot tear fell on my face, and Barbro smiled and wiped it away. "But you're safe now, that's all that matters. Rest, Brion. You can think about it later. . . ."

I tried to speak, to tell her it was all right, not to go . . .

But the dream faded, and sleep washed over me like warm, scented soapsuds, and I let go and sank down in its green depths.

The next time, I woke up hungry. Barbro was sitting by the bed, looking out the window at a tree in full spring leaf, golden green in the afternoon sun. I lay for a while, watching her, admiring the curve of her cheek, the line of her throat, the long, dark lashes—

She turned, and a smile like the sun coming out after a spring rain warmed me all the way to my bandaged heels.

"I'm okay now," I said. This time the voice came out hoarse but recognizable.

There was a long, satisfying time then, of whispered words and agreeable nonsense, and as many feather-soft kisses as we could fit in. Then Manfred came in, and Hermann, and Luc, and things got a bit more brisk and businesslike.

"Tell me, Brion," Manfred said mock-sternly. "How did you manage to leave my office, disappear for half an hour, only to be discovered unconscious beside some sort of half-ape, and dressed like a wanderer from a fancy dress ball in a variety of interesting costumes, wearing a three-day beard, with twenty-seven separate and distinct cuts, abrasions, and bruises, to say nothing of second-degree burns, frostbite, and a broken tooth?"

"What day is it?" I demanded.

He told me. I had been unconscious for forty-eight hours. Two days since the scheduled hour for the invasion—and the Hagroon hadn't appeared.

"Listen," I said. "What I'm going to tell you is going to be a little hard to take, but in view of the corpse you found beside me, I expect you to do your best. . . ."

"A truly strange creature, Brion," Hermann said. "It attacked you, I presume, which would account for some of the wounds, but as for the burns . . ."

I told them. They listened. I had to stop twice to rest, and once to eat a bowl of chicken broth, but I covered everything.

"That's it," I finished. "Now go ahead and tell me I dreamed it all. But don't forget to explain how I dreamed that dead Hagroon."

"Your story is impossible, ridiculous, fantastic, mad, and obviously the ravings of a disordered mind," Hermann said. "And I believe every word of it. My technicians have reported to me strange readings on the Net Surveillance instruments. What you have said fits the observations. And the detail of your gambit of readjusting the portal, so as to shun the invading creatures into a temporal level weeks in the future; I find that of particular interest—"

"I can't know how far I deflected them," I said. "Just be sure to station a welcoming party down there to greet them as they arrive."

Hermann cleared his throat. "I was about to come to that, Brion. You yourself have commented on the deficiencies in your qualifications for the modification of sophisticated MC effect apparatus—and by the way, I am lost in admiration of the suit you have brought home from your travels. A marvel—but I digress.

"You adjusted the portal, you said, to divert the Hagroon

157

into the future. Instead, I fear, you have shunted them into a past time-level of our Zero-zero line. . . ."

There was a moment of silence. "I don't quite get that," I said. "Are you saying they've already invaded us—last month, say?"

"The exact temporal displacement, I cannot yet state. But it seems clear, Brion, that they went back, not forward. . . ."

"Never mind that," Barbro said. "Wherever they are, they are not troubling us now—thanks to your bravery, my hero!"

Everybody laughed and my ears got hot. Manfred stepped in with a comment on the fiery figure.

"A strange sensation, my friend, to meet yourself face to face. . . ."

"Which reminds me," I said in the sudden silence. "Where's the . . . ah . . . other me?"

Nobody said anything. Then Hermann snapped his fingers.

"I think I can tell you the answer to that! It is an interesting problem in the physics of the continuum—but I think it can be accepted as axiomatic that the paradox of a face-to-face confrontation of identities is intolerable to the fabric of simultaneous reality. Hence, when the confrontation occurs—something must give! In this case, the intolerable entropic stress was relieved by the shunting of one aspect of this single ego into the plane you have called null time—where you encountered the Hagroon, and embarked on your strange adventure."

"Your friend, Dzok," Barbro said. "We must do something, Manfred, to help his people in their fight against these shaggy monsters. We can send troops—"

"I fear the implications of what Brion said regarding the disposition of the discontinuity engine have escaped you, my dear," Hermann said. There was a glint of ferocious amusement in his eyes. "From the care with which he timed his operation, I should imagine that the Hagroon shuttle bearing the apparatus of destruction arrived on schedule in the Hagroon world-line—just as the timer actuated it. The Xonijeelians have nothing to fear from invading Hagroons. Our Brion has neatly erased them from the roster of the continuum's active menaces."

"Dzok was right," Manfred said sadly. "We *are* a race of genocides. But perhaps that is a law of the nature that produced us. . . ."

"And we must help the poor peoples of these sub-technical A-lines," Barbro said. "Poor Olivia, dreaming of a brighter world, and never to know it, because we selfishly reserve its treasures for ourselves—"

"I agree, Barbro," Manfred said. "There must be a change in policy. But it is not an easy thing to bring what we think of as enlightenment to a benighted world. Whatever we do, there will be those who oppose us. This Napoleon the Fifth, for example. How will he regard a proposed status as vassal of our Emperor?"

Barbro looked at me. "You were half in love with this Olivia, Brion," she said. "But I forgive you. I am not such a fool as to invite her to be our houseguest, but you must arrange to bring her here. If she is as lovely as you say, there will be many suitors—"

"She wasn't half as gorgeous as you are," I said. "But I think it would be a nice gesture."

There was a clatter of feet at the door. A young fellow in a white jacket came in, breathing hard.

"A call for you, Herr Goering," he said. "The telephone is just here along the hall."

Hermann went out, and we talked—asking lots of questions and getting some strange answers.

"In a way," Manfred said, "it is a pity that these Hagroon were so thoroughly annihilated by your zeal, Brion. A new tribe of man only remotely related to our own stock, but having high intelligence, a technical culture—"

Hermann came back, pulling at his earlobe and blinking in a perplexed way.

"I have spoken to the Net Laboratory just now," he said. "They have calculated the destination of your unhappy party of invading Hagroon, Brion. They worked from the brief traces recorded by our instruments over the period of the last five years—"

"Five years?" several voices echoed.

"From the date on which our present improved Net instrumentation was installed," he said, "there have been a number of anomalous readings, which in the past we were forced to accept as a normal, though inexplicable deviation from calculated values. Now, in the light of Brion's statements, we are able to give them a new interpretation."

"Yes, yes, Hermann," Manfred urged. "Spare us the dramatic pause-for-effect...."

"The Hagroon, to state it bluntly, Barbro and gentlemen, have been plunged over fifty thousand years into past time by our clever Brion's adjustment to their portal!"

159

There was a moment of stunned silence. I heard myself laugh, a wild-sounding cackle.

"So they made it—just a little early. And if they tried to go back—they jumped off the deep end into an A-line that had been pulled out from under them. . . ."

"I think they did not do the latter," Hermann said. "I believe that they safely reached the Neolithic era—and remained there. I think they adapted but poorly to their sudden descent to a sub-technical status, these few hundreds of castaways in time. And, I think, never did they lose their hatred of the hairless hominids they found there in that cold northland of fifty millenia past.

"No, they were safely marooned there in the age of mammoths and ice. And there they left their bones, which our modern archaeologists have found and called Neanderthal. . . ."

THE END